SOPHIA'S LETTER

Ladies of Munro, Book 1

Elizabeth Donne

ARE YOU SIGNED UP FOR DRAGONBLADE'S BLOG?

You'll get the latest news and information on exclusive giveaways, exclusive excerpts, coming releases, sales, free books, cover reveals and more.

Check out our complete list of authors, too!

No spam, no junk. That's a promise!

Sign Up Here

www.dragonbladepublishing.com

Dearest Reader;

Thank you for your support of a small press. At Dragonblade Publishing, we strive to bring you the highest quality Historical Romance from some of the best authors in the business. Without your support, there is no 'us', so we sincerely hope you adore these stories and find some new favorite authors along the way.

Happy Reading!

CEO, Dragonblade Publishing

Additional Dragonblade books by Author Elizabeth Donne

Ladies of Munro Series
Sophia's Letter (Book 1)
Ellena's Secret (Book 2)

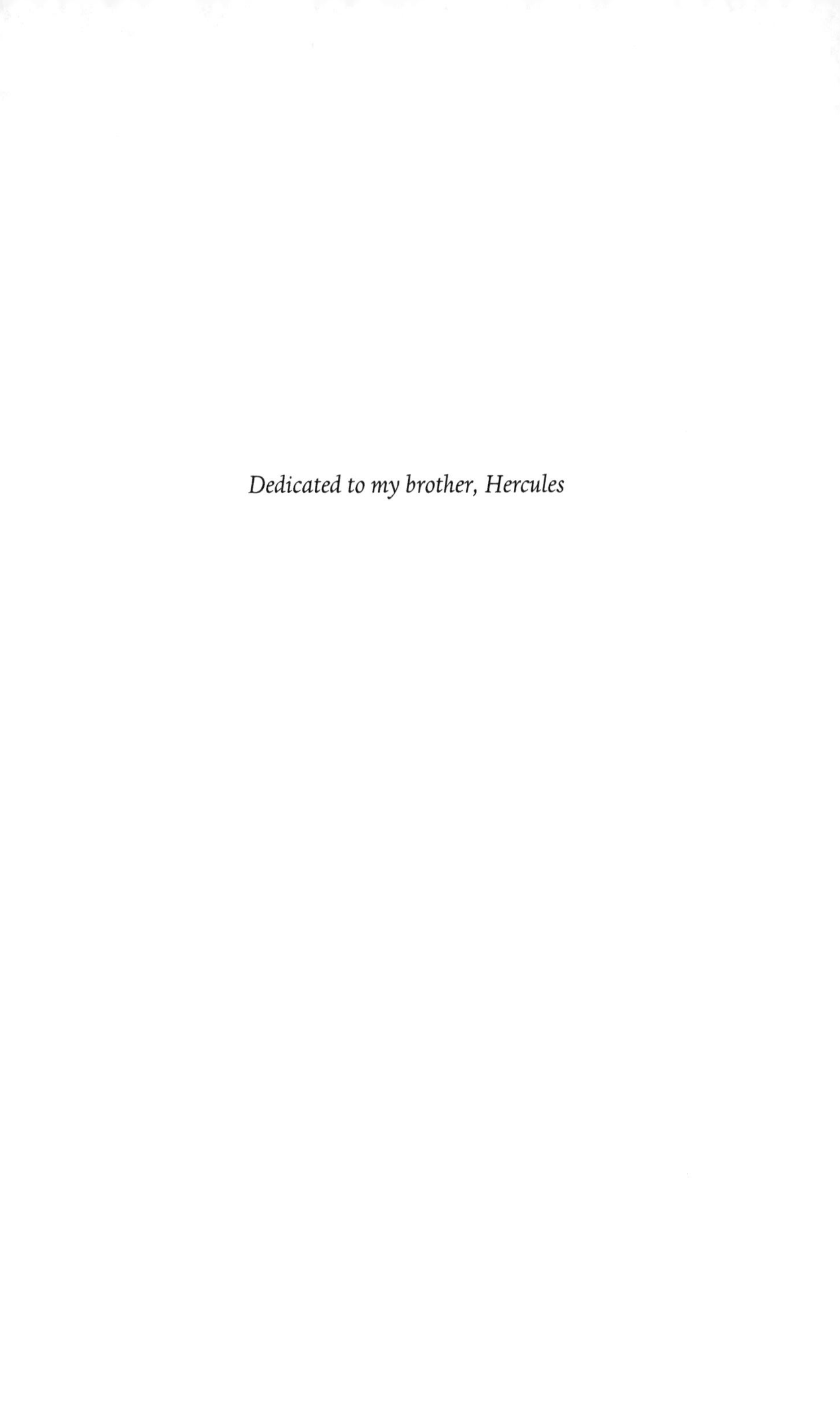

Dedicated to my brother, Hercules

CHAPTER ONE

January 1814

T HE LETTER ARRIVED on a Monday. It had not been a good day. Mondays never were. After all these years, the memory of that fateful day had still not faded into merciful oblivion. At the thought, Sophia's breathing tightened, the black silk of her bodice rising and falling in quick, shallow beats.

"Are you all right, miss?" Katie was always on alert. Sophia depended on her for the simplest things, and Katie was sharp enough to anticipate her needs. "Shall I get the smelling salts?" she asked, already reaching for them on the side table.

Sophia waved away the proffered help with an irritable hand. "I'm fine, Katie. Don't fuss." But her lady's maid still hovered. Sophia concentrated, sucking in a satisfying lungful of air. "See?" She added a thin smile. "I can manage."

She was rewarded with the girl's reluctant withdrawal to a nearby chair. A few more steady breaths and Katie's worry would subside. Sophia appreciated her vigilance, but there were times when she wished it weren't necessary.

She lay back against the arm of the chaise lounge and let her gaze fall across the room to the view outside. The sun blazed upon the snow. It was perfect weather for a walk. She imagined how the frozen path would crunch underfoot and the air would erupt with shrieks of laughter from an inevitable snowball fight.

That was denied her now. No more romping. Not in snow or autumn leaves. Not in fields of spring flowers or among the buzzing of summer insects. It had been that way for a long time. Even a slow stroll could bring on a bout of coughing and wheezing. And then Father would lay down the law, forbidding her to even sit outside among the shrubbery, lest she should catch a chill.

Mama would have found a compromise that made everyone happy.

But Mama was no more.

Sophia turned her head back to the tray of correspondence on her lap. She did not want to dwell on loss. The anxious thoughts would infiltrate her weakened body and make Katie leap from her chair again. At least her mind was still capable. Poetry and letters—*they* would fill her day. And soon, one of her siblings would look in on her. She really should not complain. There was much to be thankful for.

She spread her letters out upon the tray, her eyes searching for the writing of an unfamiliar hand. Letters from friends could wait. What she wanted most was to hear from a publisher. Papa had arranged for a book of her poems to be printed as a gift for her last birthday. And, to her delight, all the copies had been sold. But that had been Papa's doing, and at his expense. She wanted to succeed on her own merit. She ached for the recognition of the establishment, for her writing to win the approval of her literary peers.

As if in answer to her much-repeated prayer, she spotted the very thing—her name and address printed in a neat, precise hand she had not seen before. Sophia sucked in her breath, causing Katie's head to jerk up from her sewing. Sophia ignored her, snatching up the letter with eager hands. It had no formal stamp, so it was impossible to tell the name of the publisher at a glance. She pried the wax seal from the folded page and looked for the signature at the bottom.

Tobias Mannerly. She did not know a Tobias Mannerly. Perhaps he was a clerk writing on behalf of another. Well, he would say as much in his introductions. Her eyes flicked to the top of the page and she searched the opening paragraph for a name. But there was none. She caught the occasional word. *Passionate. Incomparable.*

These were not the formal words of a publisher. Indeed, these were not words that had ever been directed at her in any capacity. There must be some mistake.

She forced her racing thoughts to slow and dragged her focus back to begin the letter anew.

"My dear Miss Grant," it began. Well, that was predictable enough. And then, with a few more strokes of the quill, it was no longer so. Sophie's eyes grew wide as they took in the strange words.

> *"It is impossible to stay my hand from this page. You must be told at once. Your poems are the work of a master wordsmith. They declare themselves—and you through them—with such passionate elegance that I am loath to praise them, lest I do them an injustice with my own feeble eloquence. How other poets must hide in shame for claiming the same stage as you— you with your incomparable skill! Oh, goddess of poetry, I am your willing acolyte!"*

Sophia pressed the letter firmly back on her lap. Goodness! So much intimate prose from a stranger! What sort of man wrote such lush admiration to a woman he had not met? Surely the gentleman must know how unseemly his attention would appear?

Her brows drew together suspiciously. Was it a joke? She thought of Henry's friends at Cambridge who loved a bit of mischief. No, it couldn't be. Her brother might tease her good-naturedly when he came home for the holidays, but he would not let his friends make a mockery of her. Besides, her family knew what her writing meant to her. They would never let it be the subject of banter, let alone a prank.

She had a good mind to crumple up the page and throw it on the fire. Mr. Mannerly could not expect a different fate for his audacious sentiments. It was just as well Papa was not home. What would he say to such a letter? *Hmph.* No doubt he would think she had somehow encouraged it. There were bound to be strong words—from his side, at least. He would never tolerate her having an admirer. It was bad enough that she corresponded with academics. But at least he knew them to be old, bespectacled, and—most importantly—married. This letter—she blushed at the very thought of it—embodied a youthful vigor he would never approve of.

Sophia's private rant pulled up short. She glanced down at the offending sheet with new eyes. Papa would not like her to have it. And Papa ruled her life. She was not like Adriana, who spoke to him with unflinching boldness. Sophia hated confrontation. Illness and sorrow had taken the fight out of her completely. But she had been something of a fireball in her childhood years. Now she missed the way her high spirits had made her feel alive.

A tiny thrill ran through her.

Perhaps, after all, she should keep the letter, though its contents may be so much nonsense. Just having such a taboo possession would be a...a secret rebellion. Knowing she owned something that would infuriate her father—without the consequences of his anger—was oddly exhilarating.

In fact, she decided—with a bravado that could only come from her father's absence from the house—she would read the entire letter. It would be amusing. And, now that she had made up her mind that Mr. Tobias Mannerly could not be taken seriously, she might even enjoy the excessive flattery. It was not every day a woman was called a *goddess*.

A furtive glance toward the corner of the room told her Katie's attention was on her sewing. Good. She was a loyal companion, but the master of the house might frighten the truth from her. Better if she knew nothing to tell.

The page felt strangely warm to the touch when Sophia

picked it up once more, as if the heat of its author's fervor had been embossed upon the lines written there. Her cheeks flushed. She hesitated, her fingertips reaching involuntarily to touch her skin. It must be glowing. As long as Katie assumed it was the effect of the fire in the hearth, she was safe.

A delicious wave of subterfuge washed over her. She was getting away with something. It was only a small intrigue, but it was her very own, and she hugged it to herself.

Once more, she beheld the words that pulsed like a fever upon the page. This time, she drank them in—heady with the ardor of their author. And when she again reached the phrase "willing acolyte," she pressed on, ready to hear the rest.

"If you will but let me study at your feet, I would have you teach me the mystery of your muse. I have no gift for words myself, but words themselves are all that consume the hours in my day. What a privilege it would be to speak with one who has captured the wildness of thought and harnessed it without taming it, turning it to your will without breaking its raw spirit! You are, I am certain to my very core, a being with an essence most glorious. No language—not even yours—can possibly capture all that is you.

It would be my most profound honor to hear your thoughts on the great poets of history, for who can better understand them than one of their own? If you will permit me, I would ask to attend upon you at a day and hour of your choosing. I can offer little in return but my sincere thanks and what small insight I have gleaned from my devotion to books.

I await your reply with but a small pretense at patience.

Your humble servant,
Tobias Mannerly"

Sophia felt the rosy warmth drain from her face. He wanted to meet her! No, no, no, no! That must never happen! It was too terrible a notion to even consider! Not only would Papa be wild with vexation at the thought of it, but she could not bear to be seen. Mr. Mannerly thought her to be a glorious thing. He was clearly exaggerating in an effort to compliment her. But, even allowing for this fact, his expectations were completely at odds with reality. What would he think when he came upon her, pale and thin, and bound to her sofa? Though his effusive flattery was pure fantasy, it was a fantasy she rather wanted to cling to.

He must be discouraged from any notion of meeting. That much was certain.

She hesitated. New, unbidden feelings had begun to stir in her breast. As long as she kept him at a distance…perhaps…perhaps she need not dissuade him from writing again. Sophia touched the page gingerly, its contents electrifying her fingertips. Still, it was only a letter, wasn't it? She corresponded with several gentlemen on the topics of classical languages and the art of writing. Why should she not do so with Mr. Mannerly? She could insist that they stick to matters of literary interest.

Having made up her mind, she drew a new sheet to the center of the tray and dipped her quill into the ink. She would keep it short and formal. A few sentences would do. The quill scratched rapidly across the page, filling line after line and then ceasing abruptly. With the ink still wet, she shifted the page aside to dry and took up the original letter. She turned it over, looking for the address.

Newcliffe Hall.

That couldn't be right. Newcliffe Hall was home to the Earl of Carthige. He was famously reclusive. Tobias Mannerly was unlikely to be a visitor there. But he could scarcely be a servant— not if he could write so well and had the means to satisfy his thirst for books. He was enough of a somebody to believe that her father would permit him entry to their home and access to his daughter. But who, nay, *what* was he?

Adriana would know. She flitted about in society, much to their father's disgust. *Her* world was not limited to four walls and a maidservant. Sophia would find a way to ask her sister about Mr. Mannerly. And she would do so without divulging her secret letter.

Once again, her heart began to race, but it was a pleasant sort of thumping, like the galloping of a horse, free of constraint, with distant, unknown fields opening up before her. And, for the first time in many years, a Monday was filled with promise.

THE OLD LIBRARY was cold. It was a reminder that the room had never been intended as a library in the first place. It was on the wrong side of the house for a start, leaving the ancient pages exposed to damp and mold.

Many of the shelves were empty now. He was grateful that his uncle had listened to him, agreeing to move the collection to a warmer position better suited to preserving such precious works. Edmund Stopford was a man of culture, but his father before him had sought prey rather than prose, spending his time hunting all manner of quarry—including poachers. The family's vast collection of books had been relegated to this obscure corner of the house, miraculously surviving a generation of stubborn disinterest.

Edmund Stopford, the latest Earl of Carthige, was a learned man and a great disappointment to his father. Ultimately, he had offered the final insult by having no heir, leaving his younger brother, a foppish man even more despised by their father than studious Edmund, to one day inherit the title and estate.

There had been a daughter too. Not that it mattered. Tobias was her son, a well-bred gentleman with no great fortune. His Uncle Edmund had recognized a kindred spirit and taken him under his wing. Thus, for the past several months, Tobias had found himself carting armloads of long-forgotten books into his uncle's comfortable study, where the two men would devour the contents, catalogue the volumes, and re-home them in the new library.

Today, however, Tobias lingered among the drafty shelves of the old library, uncomfortable as it was. He wanted a few minutes to himself before setting to work on the next batch of books. In his hands, he held a letter—one he was both eager and nervous to open. *She* had written back. Regardless of what the letter said, it would be in her own hand, and her words addressed solely to him.

His uncle had warned him not to expect too much. The Grant family did not welcome strangers into their circle. Merely writing to her, uninvited, had been a risk. His uncle had told him as much. But Tobias, as usual, had rushed in where angels feared to tread. An invitation to their home was unlikely to be forthcoming. But Tobias had insisted on asking. What did he have to lose? If there was even the remotest chance that he might speak with the genius behind that sublime poetry… Well, he could but hope.

His hands shook a little as he opened the single page, his heart pounding in his ears. A few lines swam into focus. Oh, so very few! This did not bode well.

Dear Sir,

She had not even addressed him by name. Hope no longer supported him, and he sank into a nearby chair.

I thank you for your generous praise, though I fear it is not deserved. Perhaps, since you are so well-read, you would be willing to offer me helpful criticism, so that I may strive to earn the accolades you have heaped upon me. Correspondence of this nature would be most welcome.

Yours faithfully,
Sophia Grant

Tobias stared blankly at the page. She had completely misunderstood him. What possible criticism could he offer? Her writing was perfection!

Could he have offended her in some way? Why else would

her reply be so starched? Where, in all his lavish praise, could she have felt slighted?

He had done it again—created distance where he sought connection. All his years at Harrow and Cambridge had taught him everything about Greek, Latin, and French, but nothing about women. They were an obscure subject that he seemed quite unable to master. His uncle was no help to him in this regard, being something of a hermit when not forced to attend Parliament.

His hapless attempt at communicating his intentions had driven Miss Sophia Grant into hiding. Where had he failed? He tried to remember his words, every single one of them admiring and sincere. Line upon line of full-throated…

Oh. Oh dear.

He had come on too strong. He had said absolutely everything he was thinking. It had been too much.

He groaned, burying his face in his hands. She had drawn a line in the sand, and rightly so. He must have sounded like some drooling puppy. What an awful first impression he had made! He had only wanted to make her understand how masterful her writing was, what a gift it was to their generation.

Instead, she sought criticism. That was all very well. All great artists wanted to hone their craft. But what was he—a simple lover of beautiful words—supposed to add that she had not already thought of? And yet, if he hoped to correspond with her, that was the requirement.

He could not waste such a precious opportunity. Any communication with the talented Miss Grant should be grabbed with both hands. Although…*er*…perhaps grabbed somewhat more *lightly* this time.

There were no writing tools in this chilly mausoleum of a room. Taking the woeful letter up to his chambers, he set about his reply. It did not come to him immediately. As he pondered the right thing to say, he chewed upon the end of the quill, a habit that had driven his masters at Harrow to distraction.

Minutes passed and no inspiration came to him. But he must say *something*. Unconvinced that his current attempt would fare better than his last, he penned the best response he could manage.

Dear Miss Grant,

The task you have assigned me is unenviable. How am I to judge your writing when I am no writer myself? It would be the height of hubris. And if, as a reader, I am to say where you are lacking, I can only declare that there are too few of your works and I am unsatisfied to have nothing new of yours to savor.

Perhaps you would consider sharing with me a new project in the making? I might have useful advice where your thoughts are not yet fully cemented and your words not yet polished to perfection. As for your published works, I fear it is too late. Nothing can be done for them but to admire them unreservedly.

Yours most sincerely,
Tobias Mannerly

The letter was passed to the footman to be delivered with the utmost urgency. If Miss Grant were kind, she would reply this day still and put him out of his misery. She must surely be kind. He did not imagine someone who wrote so exquisitely could be anything but an angel.

But he had been wrong before.

CHAPTER TWO

A{DRIANA FLOUNCED INTO} the room and threw herself upon Sophia's bed, her curls—short and dark, like her sister's—bouncing as she did so.

"Freddy is a coward!" she announced to Sophia, who was sitting up in bed and reading a book, or trying to. Adriana sighed and rolled onto her back, staring dreamily at the ceiling. "I do love him so. Why can he not be a man and stand up to Papa? What is the worst that can happen?"

Sophia closed her book. Once Adriana had started on the topic of Freddy, she was as relentless as a bulldog.

"I think we both know exactly what would happen, Deedee," Sophia replied quietly, using her sister's childhood nickname to soften the severity of the unspoken truth.

Adriana sat up at once, her eyes wide, her youthful cheeks flushed. "He wouldn't, really. Would he, Fee? Not to family! Not after he lost Mama!"

Sophia shook her head, her expression grim. "If you marry Freddy, you will not be family anymore. Not to Papa."

"Well, I don't care!" Adriana lied. "Freddy loves me, and I love him. And if Papa is going to be mean about it, he doesn't deserve to have me for a daughter."

"Deedee! You can't mean that!"

"I can, and I do," Adriana replied sulkily, crossing her arms.

"I'm already four and twenty, Fee. I want to have a home of my own. I want children. Papa should not deny me that. I know Freddy isn't wealthy, but he is a gentleman of good character. Any other father would be happy to have him as a son-in-law."

Sophia lowered her eyes. She knew her sister was right. The things she wanted were all quite reasonable. Her own situation was different. At fourteen, she had been forced to make peace with a future as an old maid. With her thirtieth birthday just around the corner, the reality of that future was now confirmed. But Adriana had not had the paralysis fever. She was not confined to a bed or chair. She had much to offer. And a full life to live.

Instead, their father was determined to keep his children around him. He had always been a difficult man—something Mama had managed to tame to some degree with tact and subtle manipulation. Yet even at his most stubborn, he had never been cruel. Mama's death had changed him, made him hard and unyielding. And blindly possessive. He would never again give someone up. He saw in each of his five children an echo of his wife, and he would not be parted from any of it.

At first, they had tried to reason with him, reminding him that a bride or groom might be persuaded to stay in the family home. But even this did not change his mind. His children could neither alter his thinking, nor understand it fully. It became a shameful secret they were all forced to share. In time, when Bess did not come out in society, the world would know. Then again, perhaps it would not matter, since they so seldom moved within that world.

Though the years had brought a measure of understanding of their father's behavior, it had not made it easier to live with. Their brothers—knowing a young wife was always available to them no matter how old they grew—were willing to wait until their father passed on to defy his will. For Sophia, Adriana, and young Bess, the situation was more complicated. Well, Sophia had to admit, really only for Adriana. Bess had scarce been a babe when Mama had died. Now, at fifteen, she wasn't quite ready yet to enter society, even if Papa would let her. As for herself...Sophia looked at her long, pale fingers. They would only ever hold books and pens. No man would want to take her limp body into his arms. No, when it came to his eldest, their father had nothing to worry about.

"If you leave," Sophia said in a small voice, "I shall not be able to see you again. Our brothers are studying and working and living full lives. And Bess is too young to grasp the finality of my situation. Who would be left to comfort me if I lost you?"

"Oh, Fee!" Adriana flung her arms around her. "I would never leave you! You must come with me. Freddy wouldn't mind."

Sophia gave a wry laugh. "Freddy will barely be able to support you. And there will no doubt be a string of noisy little Freddies and Deedees to take care of. I would only be a burden. I cannot allow it."

Adriana was silent. Sophia knew this did not mean the end of the argument. Her sister had merely grown thoughtful. That did not bode well. Adriana's personality was spontaneous and bright. She dealt with all challenges head-on, including their father. She argued fiercely and passionately where Sophia would have shrunk within herself. If Adriana went quiet without having won the debate, it meant she was plotting a more creative way to succeed. Yet, even though Sophia knew this, she was wholly unprepared for what came next.

"I shall have to find you a husband."

Adriana said it with such solemnity that Sophia was momentarily struck mute. Then anger boiled up.

"That is not funny!"

"I did not say it in jest."

"Then you have lost your wits! You know full well there is no dowry in the world that could make a match for me. And if such a sum existed, our father would not pay it."

"Well, there is that. Papa's selfishness really does complicate matters."

"That is the least of it. Husbands want wives who are healthy and can bear them an heir. I can barely walk across the room! Really, Adriana, if I didn't know you loved me, I would think you are being cruel to even speak of marriage for me."

"But you deserve it just as much as the rest of us, dear Fee! You are clever and beautiful and thoughtful and…"

"That is irrelevant," Sophia interrupted. "There are many such ladies who also play piano and ride and show off their accomplishments. What is the point of a beautiful bride if a man cannot parade her upon his arm?"

"You are very negative," Adriana complained.

"But I am right."

Adriana sighed. "Yes," she conceded reluctantly, "you are right." The fight seemed to drain from her. "I wish you weren't. You should be happy."

"You make me happy." Sophia smiled bravely.

"But if I leave…"

"I will manage."

"You will be lonely."

"I will have Katie for company."

"*Hmph*. She is not enough. You need someone to spar with, dear sister, lest you withdraw even further into the dark corners of your mind. Someone like that Mr. Mannerly, with whom you correspond so frequently."

"Oh, *him*," scoffed Sophia. "We merely discuss my writing." Her heart fluttered a little, but it was hidden in her bosom, safe from view.

Her sister gave a look both mischievous and indignant, a look only Adriana could manage.

"Ah, yes," she said with a knowing nod, "you think me a simpleton. You use the word 'merely' when there is no such thing. I see with what eagerness you await his letters."

"I don't know what you mean!" Sophia said a little too loudly. "He is a perfectly decent gentleman with whom I discuss literature. And he is not the first."

"No, but he is young, younger even than yourself by several years. And his uncle is an earl. If Papa did not have such ridiculous notions about us marrying, he would be arranging the engagement himself." She grinned, an action which infuriated Sophia.

"There is nothing to it!" she almost shouted, which only caused Adriana's grin to widen.

"I think we should have him 'round to dinner one evening."

Sophia relaxed and leaned back against her pillows. "Well, now I *know* you are joking. You had me concerned for a moment."

"Oh, but I wasn't joking in the least." Adriana threw up a hand defensively as Sophia made to swipe her with a pillow. "Wait! Hear me out!"

"No, indeed, I shall not. You have never used those words but as a preface to some harebrained scheme, which I want no part of."

"I think you will like this one."

"No, Adriana! Even if I were comfortable inviting Mr. Mannerly to our home—which I am not—Father would take one look at him and forbid me to ever write to him again."

"Ah, so you *do* like him. Why else would it matter if your correspondence ended?"

Sophia pursed her mouth primly. "He has worthwhile commentaries on my writing."

"Oh, pooh! You have written to such men before. They carry your esteem, but not your affection. I can see the difference, you know. There has been a glow about you ever since his letters started. It's obvious to anyone with eyes."

"It is?" Sophia was horrified. "Do you think Papa has noticed?"

"No doubt he has. Though it is unlikely he has made the connection between your girlish blushes and the letters. Not yet, anyway."

"This is terrible! He mustn't!"

"So, you admit I am right? Mr. Mannerly means more to you than mere academics?"

Sophia felt the heat of embarrassment flood through her body. "It seems I am no good at keeping my own secrets."

"Truly, I am hurt that you even *have* secrets from me," Adriana protested. "Why, when you know all about Freddy?"

Sophia laughed. "Freddy is no secret. Even Papa knows about him. Honestly, Deedee, you haven't even *tried* to be subtle to keep the peace."

"I suppose that is true." Her sister shrugged. "I don't like to be silent in the face of injustice. And Papa just sets me off."

"Deedee." Sophia's voice was serious now. "You must restrain yourself. For my sake. I am not a fighter like you. If Father finds out that Mr. Mannerly makes me feel…well…*anything*, that will be the end of it. I shall be quite devastated. Do you understand? You are not to cause a scene on my behalf. Promise me."

There was a long pause. Adriana appeared to be wrestling with herself. Finally, she nodded. "All right. I agree. On one condition."

Sophia was almost afraid to ask. "What is it?"

"Papa will be going to London in the spring. He will be away for several weeks. And we will invite Mr. Mannerly and my darling Freddy to dinner." She put up a hand to stop Sophia's cry of dismay in its tracks. "Either you don't like young Mr. Tobias Mannerly and then it doesn't matter what Papa thinks. Or you *do* like him, and then, my dear sister, you should at least meet him. That is what normal people do. And for once, we are going to behave like normal young ladies. We will have our brothers here as chaperones. It will all be very proper and, I daresay, very pleasant."

Sophia groaned. She sank lower onto her bed and pulled a pillow over her face. From beneath its down-filled bulge came a dissatisfied mumble.

"This is extortion."

Adriana reached down and gently peeled the pillow back until she could see Sophia's scowling eyes.

"Call it what you like, but I'm doing this for your own good. You can thank me later."

And then, as if nothing had happened, Adriana left the room, swinging her arms happily and humming a tune Sophia did not recognize. Probably some romantic ditty their father would despise.

CHAPTER THREE

ABSOLUTELY NOTHING ON Earth could have prepared Tobias for the letter that came. He burst into his uncle's study and waved the page about like a victory banner, which, for all intents and purposes, he felt it was.

"We've been invited! Actually invited! And for dinner, no less!"

The Earl of Carthige carefully removed his glasses with his long, elegant fingers, and placed them on the desk in front of him. He was a meticulous, methodical man, and everything was done in a way that reflected this.

"Dinner, you say?" he inquired with a minimum of interest. His mind was no doubt still on the page he had been forced to abandon.

"With the Grants!"

The lack of response should not have surprised Tobias. His uncle did not like to "endure the dull rituals of society," as he called them—referring to anything that took him from his deep-seated fascination with books and art. A museum was more likely to receive a visit from him than a neighbor. Tobias imagined that, for a moment, his uncle had to recall who the Grants *were*.

At last, clarity seemed to have dawned.

"Ah, yes, the Grants. Lovely people. I remember now. You are corresponding with the eldest daughter. A poet, is she not? A worthwhile endeavor. Good for her." He reached for his glasses.

Tobias tried to suppress his exasperation. "Yes, Uncle. We have been writing each other for some weeks now. But she would not even speak of a meeting before. And now this. Dinner! I mean, it's wonderful, but only to happen in the spring. Why wait so long? What has changed? And yet not changed enough for the invitation to apply at once? I am happy, of course, but also at a loss as to how to interpret her intentions. I must say, it is far easier to understand her as a poet than a person."

He stopped to catch his breath.

His uncle stared at him as if he were a wild creature. Even worse, a wild creature set loose among his books. The horror and fascination were equal upon his face.

"Quite," was all the earl could manage. He looked with increasing urgency at the open book from which he had already been parted for too long.

"You will come with, won't you, Uncle?"

The look of horror returned. "To a dinner? With people?"

Tobias sighed. "Yes, that is the general idea."

"No-o, I don't think so."

Tobias's face fell.

The earl seemed to take pity on him. "Of course, you must go ahead and enjoy yourself without me."

"I couldn't possibly go without you," gasped Tobias. "They are strangers to me. It is likely they have only extended the invitation to me because you were their intended guest, and I am merely being included."

"You couldn't be more wrong, dear boy. They have been my neighbors for many years, but even that is a stretch of the definition. It is a good twenty minutes by carriage between our properties. I seldom venture out, as I am sure you know all too well. And Mr. Grant, as I have explained, keeps his family to himself. We do not truly know each other. It is more a case of knowing *of* each other. As such, I am more a stranger to them than you are, since you have corresponded regularly with Miss

Grant. It is more likely they have politely included me, knowing I would refuse, to enable them to invite you, the true object of their attention."

Tobias wasn't sure how he felt about being the object of someone's attention. Why did his uncle have to say it like that? His emotions were already a mess. Letters to Miss Grant were the most stressful part of his week—as much a burden to write as hers were a delight to receive. Her prose was as exquisite as her poetry. And so much of her character shone through her words. It was absolutely mesmerizing. But he never allowed himself to stray from the designated path. As instructed, he kept his replies on topic. And the topic was always the same. Miss Grant was relentless in her ambition to improve upon her writing. He did not know how to convince her that it was simply not possible. She was already at the apex of her talent. And what a talent it was!

And yet, behind the flawless lines of her letters, something else was revealed—a woman of candor, curiosity, humor—even sporadic moments of pure mischief! And always, like a dark undercurrent, the fear.

At first, he had assumed it was a form of modesty, concern that her work was somehow lacking. But though they had relaxed in their discourse, and she had come to trust his opinion, the whispering fear remained. Perhaps it was because he had—he really couldn't help himself—hinted at a visit on more than one occasion. Whether that had made her uncomfortable, he couldn't say for certain. She hadn't even acknowledged his subtle references, and he had not insisted.

It had been growing difficult not to insist. Each passing week made him more dissatisfied with their correspondence. He felt he was getting to know her, in spite of the restrictions she had placed. Surely, a meeting was the logical next step?

And if she *was* so afraid of him attending upon her in person, why the sudden invitation to dinner? And why only a month or two hence? Tobias could not make heads or tails of it.

Well, he decided, she had opened Pandora's Box. If she could change her mind about them meeting, he could change the rules also. He would simply come out and ask her directly for an explanation. If they were to be friends—for whom else do you invite to dinner?—he must be able to speak to her in a straightforward manner.

And that was where his confidence failed him. He sat down abruptly, causing his uncle to look up at him through his glasses, his finger holding the place to which he clearly hoped to return in a moment.

"Was there something else, Tobias?"

"Miss Mary Dunbar," Tobias said simply.

"Ah." The earl sat back, peeling his glasses from his slender nose once more. "I see."

"Exactly."

"Well, this is different, is it not?"

"Is it, though?" Tobias was miserable. "I was a complete blockhead when I attempted to further our acquaintance. I thought the interest was mutual."

"So you did.'"

"And I wore my heart on my sleeve."

"I remember."

"She didn't like that."

"It was unfortunate."

"And she wasn't very nice about it."

"I believe that is where the similarity ends, Tobias."

"You do?" He lifted his hanging head, his natural optimism returning with his uncle's encouragement.

"Certainly. Miss Dunbar was less than subtle about her feelings. She took pains to make a fool of you. It was most unbecoming of a lady. I do not sense such callousness in Miss Grant. She is far more likely to draw back and break contact with you than to have all her friends laugh at your expense."

"I hope you are right," Tobias said aloud. Silently, however, he prayed that she would never feel the need to distance herself utterly. An angrily worded letter he could counter. But a lasting silence from Miss Grant would be his undoing. The weight of this thought lodged itself in the pit of his stomach. The hurt Miss Dunbar had caused him could never compare. Wounded pride was no match for a broken heart.

"If there is nothing else…" The earl tilted his head toward his book, where his finger rested patiently in the same spot.

"Thank you, Uncle. If it is all right with you, I will reply to Miss Grant's letter before resuming my duties in the library."

"Yes, yes," came the reply, a wave of the hand dismissing Tobias, who retreated to his chambers.

Emboldened by his uncle's reassurance, he readied his quill with ink and laid his questions before his hostess-to-be. What had changed her mind? Could they not meet sooner? It did not have to be a dinner.

He scribbled furiously, emptying his heart of all that strained to be heard. When it was done, he read it over. It was a good letter. Forthright. Reasonable.

But in his mind's eye, he saw the veil of fear draw across her imagined face once more. He could not put his finger on its cause, yet he knew this letter would stir it up. That was not what he wanted. What sort of friend would he be if she reached out a tentative hand, only to have it grabbed too forcefully?

The page was cast into the fire.

Tobias pulled a new sheet toward him.

Dear Miss Grant,

Thank you for the kind invitation to dinner. My uncle is unable to attend, but if I will suffice, it would be my honor to accept.

Meanwhile, I have some thoughts on your most recent poem.

The pen scratched on as Tobias gave Miss Grant what she wanted. It was only in the quiet of his mind that he thought, perhaps one day, he might be permitted to give her what she needed.

CHAPTER FOUR

THAT CONFOUNDED DINNER invitation!

Sophia had tried everything to escape it. She had pleaded with Adriana. She blamed the weather, saying that spring would still be too cold for her to leave her cozy private chambers.

But Adriana was unmoved. "Was it not you who begged Papa for a carriage ride so you might take some fresh air?" Her eyebrows arched. "It would seem you have courage enough for snow, but not the hearth-heated dining room."

"You know full well the snow does not terrify me as much as our father's wrath," Sophia countered.

Her sister shrugged. "Papa need never know. We have become quite adept at sneaking off on our little adventures behind his back."

"You don't even bother sneaking," Sophia grumbled. "And I have only ever been a secret *keeper*. I have never created one of my own."

Adriana's lips tweaked into a poorly concealed smile. "Except for Mr. Mannerly."

"Keeping our correspondence secret wasn't my choice."

"You are a poor liar, Fee. You could easily have discarded Mr. Mannerly's letters. He would soon have given up trying. But you love every word he has written. Why, I am amazed the pages haven't fallen to shreds from your constant re-reading of them!"

"You shouldn't spy on me." Sophia pouted. "It is poor form."

"Just admit it. You can't wait to meet him."

Sophia hesitated. There was a degree of curiosity, to be sure. What did Mr. Mannerly look like? How did his voice sound?

But far, far deeper than this superficial interest ran the vein of fear. Her father was a surprisingly small part of it. What truly turned her blood cold was the thought of dear Mr. Mannerly discovering that the pedestal he had placed her on was made only of words. When reality leaned too heavily upon them, they would scatter from his mind, and his admiration with them.

"No." Sophia's answer was firm. "I would do very well if I never met him. You are risking my pleasant correspondence with Mr. Mannerly to satisfy your own love of intrigue. It is not kind, Adriana."

Her sister's face clouded. "I *am* being kind. I am trying my best to leave you in good hands when I marry Freddy. Or do you not want me to be happy? Perhaps it is *you* who are unkind. Perhaps you would like to see me shrouded in this house along with you, turning ever more gray and wrinkled until one of us abandons the other to death…"

"Dee-Dee!" Sophia's hands flew to her mouth. "Don't say such things!" Tears pricked her eyes. "I would never want you to share my fate."

Adriana's momentary disgruntlement dissolved. She lowered her head in shame. "I'm sorry. I went too far. Perhaps I take after our father more than I'd like."

"Papa was not always as he is now."

"No. He had better qualities. And I should emulate those. I should be looking out for you." Adriana lifted her eyes to her sister once more. "I'm trying my best, Fee. I really am."

Sophia released a heavy sigh. "I'm not sure this dinner is going to achieve what you wish it to. In fact, I am quite convinced of the opposite."

A warm hand touched Sophia's arm. "That is only because you don't see yourself as we do. Mr. Mannerly is going to be more smitten than ever. He will want to carry you off with him the moment he lays eyes on you." Adriana's voice once again took on its familiar teasing ring. "Shall I order the footmen to hold him down when he does?"

It was impossible to reason with Adriana. She was not afraid to claim what was due her, or demand it on behalf of those she loved. And she assumed the rest of the world would make room for her, especially if she stood, legs akimbo, hand on hip, waggling her finger at it.

Acknowledging defeat against her sister's stubborn optimism, Sophia considered another possible source to assist her in canceling the dinner. It couldn't be Henry. He was still away at Cambridge. And Adriana was too bold a force for him to argue with her in a letter. It was hard enough to reason with her face to face.

Of course, Adriana would make sure Henry attended the dinner. When Father was away, the five siblings made a point of spending time together. The mood that reigned then harkened back to happier times. Almost as if Mama were still with them. Certainly, Adriana would call Henry home for a visit the moment Father left. But for now, he was unavailable to strengthen Sophia's cause.

George would be no help, either. Adriana had too much with which to blackmail him. They all hid things from their father. The secrets ranged in severity, from George's white lie about a work commitment so that he could spend a few days in London, out from under their father's iron thumb, to the apocalyptic truth that Adriana was already engaged to Freddy.

That just left Bess. She was too young to undermine their father's will, so Adriana had no secrets to hold over her. But she was also too young to have developed any skills that might challenge their brazen middle sister.

No, there was nothing for it. If Sophia was going to escape this dreaded dinner, she would have to reach for the only weapon she had.

Her father's love.

It had become a strange, flightless version of the soaring devotion it once was—a twisted thing, corrupted by a sense of loss he had been unable to overcome. But the love was still there at his core.

Her health concerned him. Not in the possessive way that had soured much of his relationship with his children, but as a genuine worry for the wellbeing of his favorite child. Using it against him felt wrong. She just didn't know what else to do.

Papa would not go to London if she were ill. And, if he did not leave, the dinner would be called off. It was a desperate act. And it was guaranteed to work. So, Sophia played the one ace she had. She took to her bed.

No sooner had Katie plumped up the pillows behind her than Papa materialized at her side. His dark, haunted look was exaggerated further with concern. His oiled queue had released a strand, which fell forward as he leaned toward her, arm extended.

"Should I send for the doctor?" he asked, touching the back of his hand to her feverless forehead.

"No, Papa. There is no need. I am just tired."

"You should not walk so much," he said with more concern than rebuke. "Katie must bring you what you need. And a footman is always available to carry you."

"I know, Papa. I merely stand to be dressed. I have no opportunity to exert myself." Her statement carried an edge of complaint, which her father seemed not to hear.

"Then it must be an illness." He straightened up, furrows of worry etched upon his forehead. "I will send for Doctor Wesley at once."

Sophia tried to harden her heart. Her father had brought this upon himself. She would not have to go to such extreme lengths if Mr. Mannerly had been welcome in their home. The dinner would have been easy to arrange, and then...

And then Mr. Mannerly would see her as she was. And those letters that brought her so much joy would swiftly change. Oh, he would be polite about it, she had no doubt. But they would wane into mere academic correspondence. In truth, it was all she had asked for. But Mr. Mannerly had been wonderfully persistent in his adoration of her. It was clear he had tried to curb his enthusiasm for her sake, yet it permeated every letter despite his best efforts. She could no longer imagine her life without his admiration, misplaced though it was.

She tried to ignore the pain in her father's eyes. This once, she was putting herself first. Papa would never leave her now. Not after he had done so on that Monday fifteen years ago. He owed her this much.

He would stay with her this day, this week, this month. Whatever it took.

A trickle of stark reality ran like icy water through her thoughts. How long was she willing to confine herself to her bed? How would her father conduct his business if he never tended to it in London? Mightn't Mr. Mannerly discover the truth about her through a gossipy neighbor instead?

If he came to dinner… If she saw the disappointment in his eyes… At least she would have seen him. It was small consolation. Under the circumstances, perhaps she should be grateful there was any. Best to get it over and done with. No Doctor Wesley fussing over her, guessing at what medicine might relieve her mysterious malady. No Papa fretting by her bedside. No prison to be made from her bedroom.

"I am merely feeling sorry for myself," she confessed as her father hovered over her. "It would be selfish of me to keep you home when you have important business in London. I have such good care here, and I am feeling better already. It is just a passing melancholy."

His obvious relief when she appeared to perk up soon afterward ate at her conscience. She had toyed with the one part of him that was still pure, all because she couldn't face her own fears regarding a gentleman with whom she had no future. It made her more miserable than ever. Her father would still go to London.

Mr. Mannerly would still come to dinner. She had hurt her father for nothing.

PAPA LINGERED A little by Sophia's side the morning before he left. "You are certain nothing ails you?"

"No more than what is usual," she answered bravely, lifting her chin and offering him a smile. "There is no need for you to worry, Papa. I am as well as I can be."

Her father must have accepted her at her word, for he kissed her gently on her forehead. "I'll be back in just a few weeks."

"Perhaps then it will be warm enough for us to take the carriage and see a bit of the countryside," she added hopefully.

Her father frowned. "We shall see."

If she had been Adriana, she would have folded her arms stubbornly and retorted smartly, *"We certainly shall."* But she was not Adriana. Instead, she waited until she heard her father's carriage leaving the drive before calling to Katie to bring her the writing tray. She had no more excuses. She was resigned to her fate.

A short letter to Mr. Mannerly provided the date and time for dinner. She didn't have the will to discuss poetry. All her energy was spent on keeping her rising panic from overcoming her.

The letter was dispatched. And Sophia waited in agony.

Oh, if only he would be too busy! But, as she had expected, the reply was immediate and a resounding "yes." In two days, Mr. Mannerly would be here. And it would at last be clear to him— the proof irrefutably before him—that she was by no means a goddess. And the pedestal he had placed her on would crumble to dust.

CHAPTER FIVE

A FIRE BLAZED in the dining room, and extra rugs and cushions were brought to make Sophia as comfortable as possible. But nothing could ease the pounding of dread that thrummed within her. By the time the footman had shown their guests in, she was almost paralytic with fear.

She barely greeted Freddy, who kissed her on the cheek as if she were already his sister. But Sophia had no time to ponder whether that would ever be a reality, because Mr. Tobias Mannerly entered shortly on Freddy's heels.

He approached hesitantly, his eyes searching the small crowd assembled there. All had risen to acknowledge him except Sophia, who was rendered motionless with both physical weakness and self-doubt.

His gaze found her at last, and his entire being lit up. He was shorter than she had imagined, but he strode across the floor toward her with a briskness that belied his height.

"Miss Grant!" he breathed, as if in the presence of inspiring beauty. "At last!"

His eyes shone, and his lips were red with a rush of feeling. He seemed oblivious of her faded looks, her body that would not let her rise to greet him properly. How grateful she was now that Katie had fussed over her hair. It was the one part of her, other than her mind, that still did what it was told. She lifted her hand to a dark tendril that draped at her neck and murmured shyly, "It is good to see you."

"Well, that is one introduction complete," teased Adriana. "Shall we make short work of the rest?" Without waiting for an answer, she nodded to George to do the honors. When he was done, she lightly touched Mr. Mannerly's shoulder and indicated the empty chair next to Sophia. "Mr. Mannerly, won't you be seated?" she said before turning to take Freddy by the arm.

"You have the place beside mine." Adriana smiled. In truth, it was much more than a smile, for in that one look, she was offering Freddy her heart.

Sophia had to admit, she was envious of Adriana. Envious that it all came so easily to her. For when Mr. Mannerly lifted his coattails to sit, all she could offer him was uncomfortable silence.

A soft murmur of polite conversation began as the Grant siblings bid welcome to their guests. Soon the chatter around the table grew lively. But Sophia remained apprehensive and mute.

Any moment now, it would sink in. He would register her thin limbs, the dark circles beneath her eyes. His uncle should have warned him, but perhaps he had not truly understood. Here, in her presence, the reality was unmistakable.

Tobias turned to look at her, and she shrank under his honest scrutiny.

His expression did not change. She held her breath, waiting for his smile to droop. Instead, it held.

The tiniest edge of her fear dissolved.

"I cannot tell you how pleased I am to finally meet you, Miss Grant," he said, his eyes never swerving from her face. "Of course, putting thoughts into words is no challenge for *you*. Alas, I do not share your gift. I can only hope that sincerity suffices where skill is wanting."

Sophia straightened her back. "Indeed, sir, I prize candor above all else."

"I knew you would!" he gushed. "I feel like I have come to understand you through your poems and letters. It was impossi ble that we should not become friends. You are so unlike any other woman I know!"

He stopped abruptly, his gaze dropping away just as suddenly.

"I...I am sorry. You must think me terribly forward. It is a fault I struggle to overcome." He looked up, his eyes pleading. "Please say you will not take offense. I mean no harm."

"It is quite all right," Sophia replied, surprised to find that she meant it.

His demeanor bounced back to cheerfulness instantly, a brilliant smile creasing his laugh lines. "Excellent! You are a miracle, Miss Grant! How fortunate a man I am to be acquainted with you."

Sophia was speechless. Did the man not have eyes? Clearly, he did, for they stared at her unblinkingly. Was he a fool, then? His letters had seemed intelligent enough. And yet, he persisted in admiring her.

A bowl of soup was placed before Mr. Mannerly, and he turned grudgingly toward it.

"You will forgive me, Miss Grant, but I shall have to give all my attention to the dish. I wish I were not a clumsy man, but soup has often been my undoing." He grinned sheepishly. Then, his brow furrowed in concentration, he dipped his spoon into the creamy, white liquid.

She watched him more closely now that she was free to do so without being watched in return. She was trying to reconcile the man before her with the assumptions she had made about him. His connections with nobility had thrown her, to be sure. She had imagined him to be a more worldly sort of man, mixing in all the right circles, flamboyant, even a little inclined to preen, like the younger of his two uncles. Certainly, he was dressed immaculately. And there was not a hair out of place. Not a single one of his perfect sandy-blond curls. They all fell to the side in a soft wave.

It would feel good to run her fingers through hair like that...

His lips, too, were shapely, closing about each spoonful gracefully and then firmly embracing the spoon as it was drawn slowly from his mouth.

Sophia felt a slight sweat forming in her neck. *Tch, they made the fire too hot!* She pushed the rug from her lap. It slid to the floor.

In a trice, Mr. Mannerly had reached down and collected it. He offered it back to Sophia, his face turned toward her once more. Now she could see his blue eyes. They contained none of the haughtiness she had presumed would be there. No, they were kind and open. And in them she could see a future worth having.

"Did you not want this?" he asked, still holding out the rug to her.

"Oh," she managed to say, trying to collect herself. "Oh that," she added, as if seeing the rug for the first time. It was almost impossible to tear herself away from those blue eyes that looked at her with the patient question still unanswered. "Er...the footman can take it away. I am no longer cold."

"No, indeed, your cheeks are quite flushed," he noted.

His comment made her more self-conscious, and she felt the warmth deepen upon her face.

He peered more closely at her.

"Actually, Miss Grant," he said with concern, "you seem to be developing a fever."

"I assure you, I am quite well," Sophia insisted. His focused attention only heightened her embarrassment, and she desperately willed her face not to betray her. She knew she must be quite crimson by now.

Mr. Mannerly's skin, by contrast, drained of its color. He flung the rug to the floor and grasped her hand as if to support her. "This dinner is too much for you," he said with some alarm. "You are overexerting yourself."

Several of Sophia's siblings looked up from their soup with some surprise. George opened his mouth—no doubt to protest at Mr. Mannerly's liberties—but Adriana shook her head at him urgently. George subsided, but Sophia had the feeling his soup did not receive his full attention anymore.

Meanwhile Tobias was looking at her hand, its bony, ashen form nestling in his own sturdy palm. He shook his head sadly. "It is my fault. I have badgered you for a meeting. But you knew better. You knew you would not manage. I have been selfish in my enthusiasm. I have not understood."

Sophia gingerly drew her hand from his. In the corner of her eye, she saw George exhale and relax into his chair. "You are not to blame, sir," she told Tobias. I am pleased you have come."

Of course, she meant it. The reality of his presence had been more than she could have hoped for in her private fantasies. But it was time to come down to Earth again. She pursed her lips. "Yes, it is very good that you have come. For now you can see the facts before you. You understand. I am little more than an invalid." It was a relief to pull the veil from his eyes. If they were at least to be friends, he should understand what little she had to offer. "All you knew of me before were words on a page," she continued. "My writing gives me the means to enter a world that is otherwise closed to me. In my letters, I am whole. But here you see me as I am. Weak. Confined to my chair. Easily flustered. Perhaps now you will see fit to adjust your opinion of me. At least there will be no further cause for false compliments."

There. No more pretense. Sophia was glad of it.

Then why did it stab at her heart so?

But there was no relief in the face of Mr. Mannerly. Instead, the worry turned to confusion and pain.

"False compliments?" His voice was a whisper, as if uttering the words were an offense to the ear. "You believe I have tainted my admiration of you with dishonesty?" He sat back, running his fingers through his mop of hair. Then he threw his hand up in frustration. "I know my faults, Miss Grant. I am wordy to excess. But I never exaggerate. I am sorry if you have found my praise tiresome, but it was never, ever bloated with flattery."

The hurt was so shallow in his eyes that Sophia could not bear it. She wanted to cup his face in her hands and cover it with slow, comforting kisses. He was like a child in his innocence, but in every other way, a man. A very dear man. A very lovely, lovely man.

"You did not realize your compliments were undeserved," Sophia tried to explain. "I only wish for you to alter future correspondence to reflect the reality you have discovered here tonight."

His pained features softened, but the confusion remained. "How are you different from my expectations?" he questioned. "Are you not intelligent, talented, honest, and true? How have I misjudged you?"

Sophia breathed out an exasperated sigh. "These qualities are not the whole story, sir, as you can clearly see."

"I do not see how your difficulty in walking is relevant. Would a stronger step have made you a better poet, or given you greater integrity?"

"No, I suppose not, but…"

"What am I missing? What would you have me change in my regard for you?"

Sophia blushed again. It was proving very difficult to have the man see reason. Moreover, his stubbornness was strangely comforting. She was no longer quite as motivated to alter his fond appraisal of her.

She caught a reassuring smile from her sister. Adriana was leaning slightly towards Mr. Mannerly, whose speech was too soft to travel far. Her sister was drinking in every word of their conversation, though she nodded at the rest of the company at appropriate intervals. She would likely scold Sophia later for countering Mr. Mannerly at every turn.

Sophia hesitated. Perhaps Adriana was right. Was it truly necessary to undo *all* of the kind gentleman's generous opinions?

"I certainly would not want you to think less of me than I am…" she answered at last.

"But you think I do not see you as you *really* are."

"Yes!"

He sat back, and looked at her with determined concentration.

"I see it now," he confessed at last.

"You do?" Her heart sank.

"The fault is clearly with you."

"It is?" Her chest tightened.

"It is *you* who do not see yourself as you really are."

"Oh!" She exhaled in relief.

"My dear Miss Grant, if you will permit my candor, I suspect you have been greatly disappointed by your physical limitations and therefore assume everyone feels the same. I, however, do not see how it makes one jot of difference to the person you are. All the qualities I have discovered in your letters and wonderful lines of poetry are the ones I value most. I fail to grasp how your health would improve your character, though I do sympathize that it is a frustration for you. I do not know how to make this any clearer."

It took several moments for Sophia to regain her bearings.

"I see," she said, though truly, she did not. She had spent the latter half of her life thus far mourning her losses—her health, her mother. They had robbed her of joy and freedom. The vivacious girl of her youth was gone, replaced by this old maid of nearly thirty in a body that didn't work. In contrast, young Mr. Mannerly was so full of energy, his life ripe with promise. Why was he not repulsed by her? He should have been.

"Ah, Miss Grant." He shook his head slowly. "I have not convinced you." He sighed. "Well, let us agree to disagree, then. It should not spoil the evening. After all, there is always hope for any dinner where I have not spilled soup on my napkin." He offered her a lopsided grin, and she could not help but return it.

By now, the footman was serving the roast beef, and chatter had swelled around the table. It was a remarkably genial gathering with George playing host instead of their father. Freddy and Adriana exchanged tender glances, their hands finding excuses to brush lightly past each other. Henry got away with student humor that would have been summarily condemned by their father. And Bess, who had been allowed to join the dinner despite not being out officially, was beside herself with excitement, her youthful laughter punctuating the spirited dialogue.

Sophia allowed herself to forget Mr. Mannerly's delusions for the moment. He was obdurate in his opinion of her, and she had given up persuading him otherwise. Tomorrow, they would continue their literary correspondence, and everything would return to its comfortable, predictable status quo. As it should.

And yet, when she watched him chatting with, well, *anyone* at the table, he fit right in. It was uncomplicated. Joyous even. So very, very opposite to her daily life. It brought back memories of the dinners Mama would arrange when Papa had traveled to London. She'd only done so when he'd been from home. Not because he would have spoiled the mood. No, not then. But because she'd known that, when he returned, he would want to have his family all to himself. He'd always missed them terribly and would scoop them up in his arms where they'd waited for him excitedly at the door. There would be noisy play, with their usually reserved father growling like a lion and chasing them about the house.

She barely recognized who he was now. He would not like this gathering at all. It was noisy, cheerful, and certainly not safe. How was he to keep his daughters close to home when there were such eligible gentlemen present?

Sophia wondered if Mr. Mannerly would still delight in her company if he knew how strange her family was. Well, she wasn't going to let it bother her tonight. It was just the one dinner. Papa would never find out. They all protected each other's secrets. Mr. Tobias Mannerly and Conrad Grant were much better off knowing nothing about each other.

As the evening wore on, Sophia let herself laugh. She did not stop Adriana from divulging what an absolute urchin their eldest sister had been as a child, able to outrun and out-pummel her brothers as the need had arisen. Mr. Mannerly had turned to Sophia, his mouth an "O" of surprise. But he did not appear shocked. He seemed incapable of being rattled.

By the time their guests were readying to leave, Sophia was still keeping up with the rest of the company. She felt strong, buoyant. The visit had refreshed rather than drained her. She almost wished…yes, she *did* wish it could happen again.

"You look well, Miss Grant," Mr. Mannerly said as he took his leave. "I am relieved that you have made a complete recovery from your earlier turn. May I say that the color that now touches your cheeks is most becoming?"

"You know very well you should not say such things," Sophia scolded, but her heart was no longer in it. She let him kiss her gloved hand. She would have to buy a new pair—this one would be squirreled away under her pillow, ready for her to savor the delectable memory (and the lips that had formed it) whenever she chose. She was walking on air.

Without thinking, she rose from her chair.

There was a gasp from Bess. The room went quiet. All eyes turned in Sophia's direction.

"Whatever is the matter?" she asked.

"Are you tired? Shall I have a footman carry you to your room?" inquired George with some concern.

"That is not necessary. I feel quite fit enough." Sophia felt as surprised as they looked. "Yes." A broad smile echoed her realization. "I feel…I might walk to my chambers myself if someone offered me their arm."

She was momentarily disappointed when Mr. Mannerly did not offer. It would, of course, have been inappropriate. But such was the wholesome nature of the man that she would have accepted gladly and not thought his intentions anything but honorable.

Henry, who was nearest to her of her brothers, stepped forward briskly and held his arm out to her. "Ready?" he asked, though his dubious expression suggested he did not think she possibly could be.

"Ready." She nodded. His arm stiffened as she placed some of her weight upon it. It was enough. She would manage. Sophia turned to Mr. Mannerly. "Thank you for coming." The simple words did not do justice to the impact his presence had had, but she was certain he knew this.

He bowed, his hand to his chest. "It has been…pure poetry."

It would have been a fitting response to stride from the room like a queen, gliding on the euphoria of an evening unlike any other. Instead, Sophia walked slowly, taking great care not to give the appearance of shuffling. Out of sight of Mr. Mannerly, she stopped to catch her breath.

Henry put a supportive arm around her. "Would you like to sit a while?"

"I can do it." She was panting slightly, but determined to see it through.

"Look, Fee, if anyone can do it with the power of sheer doggedness, it's you. But nowhere is it written you have to do it all at once."

"You promise not to fetch a footman?"

"I promise."

She lowered herself gratefully onto a wide bench. Henry joined her. Despite his youth, and the playfulness suggested by freckles and strawberry-blond hair, he was just as patient and sensible as George. Sophia counted her brothers among the handful of blessings that remained to her. It was easy to be herself in their company. As it was with Mr. Mannerly…

She looked down to hide the blush she felt rising to her cheeks. Her eyes fell on the small table that stood beside them. It supported a wide-lipped vase. Being early spring, there were daffodils, irises, and snowdrops on display. She wondered who had picked them. It was something she had always done with her mother. Her blush evaporated as a chilly reminder took its place. Neither her mother nor she would gather flowers again.

And it was her fault.

The well of energy that had filled up during the evening poured out of her so suddenly that she slumped against Henry.

"What's wrong?" he asked, buoying her up against his chest.

"I…I probably just overdid it."

"Too much too soon?"

"Yes, that's it. I'll be fine once I've had a proper rest."

"Say no more."

And because Henry was a good brother and would keep his promise, he reached over and scooped Sophia up into his own arms and carried her to her room.

Katie fussed while undressing her, wishing aloud that her mistress would not take such risks with her health. But Sophia was too tired to listen. She watched from her bed as the maid carefully collected her black silk dress, shoes, and other paraphernalia, to be taken downstairs and cleaned.

As her eyelids began to close heavily, Sophia murmured, just loud enough to be heard, "Leave the gloves."

CHAPTER SIX

"DEAR BOY, I hardly think that is how one goes about it."

Uncle Edmund was once again paused in his reading. The strained patience in his expression suggested it was becoming a far-too-frequent occurrence. And by frequent, it would mean anything that happened more than once.

Tobias had vacated his chair in agitation and was now pacing behind it. His uncle just did not understand. How could he? The man was a self-confessed recluse. What did he know of love? "I don't see the difficulty," he protested. "Miss Grant and I are an excellent match. Our time together last night has more than confirmed it."

"I will take your word for it," his uncle replied with a calm that infuriated Tobias. The earl cleared his throat. "*However,* that in and of itself is not sufficient. I am given to understand that such feelings should be, *ahem,* mutual."

"Well, of course they are!" Did his uncle think he was a fool? "I would hardly be proposing marriage if I did not believe the lady would welcome it!"

"Good, good. That is reassuring. Nevertheless…"

"Nevertheless what? What else is needed?" Tobias flailed in the air with his arms, then brought them down on the back of the chair to grip it with a white-knuckled ferocity. "Surely, you cannot disapprove of Miss Grant. She is above reproach!"

His uncle let out a protracted sigh and pinched the bridge of his nose where his glasses should have been. "It is not the choice of young lady that raises my concern, Nephew, but rather how you are going about wooing her. I would be the first to admit this is not my field of expertise, but I know what passes for etiquette in these matters. To my knowledge, one meeting will not suffice as preface to a proposal. I understand you haven't even met her father yet. It is just. Not. Done."

Tobias stared hard at his uncle.

Lord Carthige did not flinch.

Several animated retorts churned in Tobias's mind. Annoyingly, his uncle's single, simple argument batted these thoughts away, one by one.

Tobias's shoulders sagged. "Very well then. I will arrange another meeting. I will ask to be introduced to her father. And *then*, I will ask for her hand. Will that satisfy?"

"If you are able to obtain an interview with Conrad Grant, that will already be a notable triumph. And if you still wish to marry into that family after you have met him, I will give you my personal blessing, and"—he muttered under his breath—"my prayers."

"Thank you, Uncle. That seems simple enough."

His uncle tilted his head. "I think you will find that is not the case."

"Why do you persist in being so negative?" Tobias cried in exasperation.

"Tobias." The earl's voice took on a stern edge. "We have been down this path. You are too hasty in your declarations. And you are over abundantly optimistic in all things. There is often more to consider than you allow for."

"But…"

"No, you must hear me in this. You are rushing headlong into matters, just as you did with Miss Dunbar. The difference is that Miss Grant is actually worth waiting for. You will have to exercise tremendous restraint to secure said young lady. There is sorrow in that house that has lingered too long. It casts a shadow over everyone who resides there. If you go blundering in where angels fear to tread, she is as good as lost. I caution you out of my deep love and respect for you. You should show the same to this woman with whom you would share your life."

The rebellious fire in Tobias was doused at last. He had many questions for his uncle, but the man had already spoken more than was comfortable for him. His uncle's willingness to do so to protect him was a gift in and of itself. Tobias would not put further strain upon him. And, because he spoke true, Tobias was now wary of putting similar pressure on Miss Grant.

"Thank you for your advice, Uncle. I will do my best to reel in my enthusiasm." He breathed in deeply and let out a resigned sigh. "As you have rightly pointed out, it is my Achilles heel." His ears grew warm with embarrassment at the memory of Miss Dunbar. He could only hope that, if he stumbled into old habits, Miss Grant would be more forgiving. There was only one way to find out.

"Um, I was wondering if…"

"Yes, yes. Go and write your letter. It will be impossible for us to continue our work here until you do." Lord Carthige offered him a wry smile, but it was a smile nonetheless.

"Thank you! I won't be but a moment."

"*Hmph*," came the disbelieving reply. Tobias opened his mouth to add comment, but Lord Carthige already had his nose back in his book. His expression returned to one of serenity, all external troubles of the world forgotten.

Perhaps my uncle has the right idea, thought Tobias—life ensconced in books was safe and secure. His heart, however, was quick to contradict him. He savored an image of the wondrous Miss Grant with her dark, piercing eyes and intelligence to match. His thoughts lingered on her mouth—both sensual and serious. Ah, yes, if loving Miss Grant made life complicated, it was something he was just going to have to bear.

CHAPTER SEVEN

THE AFTERNOON POST brought the daily letter from Mr. Mannerly that Sophia now eagerly awaited and cherished. Nothing further could come of their correspondence, of course, but it was the nearest thing to intimacy she had ever allowed herself.

The hardest part was keeping from showing any excitement at the arrival of the post. With Katie always on duty, Sophia had to open all letters with equal decorum.

Today, the wail escaped her lips before she could stifle it.

At once, Katie was alert.

"Are you unwell, miss?" Her forehead was pleated with worry. Then she saw the open letter in her mistress's hand. "Not bad news, I hope?"

"No, no!" Sophia spluttered. "Of course not! I just… It's only…" Her denial ground to a stuttering halt. "Oh, Katie," she cried, "why must men be so contrary?!"

Katie took the question in her stride. "I don't know, miss. I am sure they would say the same of us." She smiled shyly. "If you'll pardon my saying so."

Sophia slumped back onto the arm of the sofa. "It was all going so well." She tapped the letter accusingly. "Why would he get such a thought in his head?"

"Begging pardon, miss, but I cannot answer the question,

seeing as I don't know who or what the mistress is talking about. Forgiving my bluntness, miss."

Sophia turned her head and looked at Katie properly for the first time. She had sharp features: cheekbones, nose, chin, all of it. And bright eyes to match. Papa would not have entrusted his precious child to a dullard, but Sophia had never really pondered this before.

"Katie," she began, her head cocked thoughtfully, "what do you do when you are not looking after me?"

"Oh, well, I make sure the mistress's clothes are clean and pressed. I tend to the fire. I…"

"No, I meant when you have time to yourself."

"To myself?" The blank look on Katie's face gave Sophia pause.

"Yes, you know, when you are not busy."

"I…I hardly know how to answer that, miss. If I am not busy, then I am not doing me job properly."

"Oh. I see. So you do not have an admirer? Someone to whom you might slip away in your stolen moments?"

Katie snort-laughed and then threw a cupped hand across her mouth, her eyes wide. "Begging your pardon, miss! I did not mean to sound disrespectful. It's just that, if the master was to think I had me a young man, I'd be sacked on the spot."

Sophia was horrified. "You could never fall in love? Never marry?"

Katie lowered her eyes, a corner of her mouth twitching into a demure smile. "I didn't say that, miss. It's just, if I did, I couldn't stay here any longer. I'd have to choose."

"I know the feeling."

"Yes, miss. Poor Miss Adriana."

"Miss Adriana?"

"Oh, yes, miss! It's so sad that she cannot have a normal courtship. They make such a lovely couple."

"You know about Fr… I mean, Mr. Wynn?"

Katie's chin lifted and her chest swelled a little. "Miss Adriana trusts me with delivering their correspondence. I always take great care not to let them down. Her beau cannot send his letters here like your Mr. Mannerly does."

Sophia's eyebrows shot up, and a warning sounded up the length of her spine.

"*My* Mr. Mannerly?"

"Yes, miss. If the mistress don't mind me saying, she's been clever not to speak of her feelings to the master. Miss Adriana is very bold, but it has also cost her dearly, 'cause now the master watches her closely and it is difficult for her to meet with Mr. Wynn. Not that it stops her. She's a brave one. All the staff are rooting for her. We all love a romance, we do."

"That is very heartening to know, I'm sure. But I would like to make it clear—Mr. Mannerly and I do *not* have a romance."

Katie tapped her nose and winked. "Of course not. I understand, Miss Grant."

"I don't think you *do*. Mr. Mannerly and I correspond about literature. Perhaps you have confused our friendship with something more. Surely, your enjoyment of a good romance should not require you to invent one?"

"Oh, Miss Grant, it's all right. I would never betray you to the master! You deserve to be happy."

Sophia felt the weight of these words. *Oh, Katie, if only you knew. I deserve nothing of the kind. Not dear Mr. Mannerly. And certainly nothing as rewarding as real happiness.*

The cold reality squeezed at her heart. But Katie had meant well, and so Sophia stirred a measure of warmth into her voice. "These are generous sentiments, Katie, and I do not take them lightly. But it must be obvious to anyone that a relationship between Mr. Mannerly and myself is quite impossible. There is nothing for you to be protective of, though your loyalty is appreciated."

"Oh, miss! If it weren't for the master, I believe you and Mr. Mannerly would be courting openly, and very happy besides. We all think he is good for you."

"Is that so? And what is it I am supposed to offer him in return, would you say, Katie Williams? Hmm?"

The sarcasm that laced her speech was completely lost on poor Katie, who blundered onward in her enthusiasm.

"He is a learned man, and you are so very clever, miss."

"That is a sound basis for friendship, not love."

The young maid shrugged. "It's not for me to say what the gentleman appreciates in you. But the way he looks at you is...not like a friend." Katie giggled, as if they were sharing a girlish secret.

Sophia did not laugh. She sat with her spine straight and stiff, her fingers knitted together on her lap. "How would you know how he looks at me?"

Katie was taken aback. "Oh...er...the footman...at the dinner..."

"You discuss us? And our guests? With the rest of the staff?"

"O-Only out of a-admiration," Katie stammered. "We would never gossip maliciously. We have all worked here for years, Miss Grant. You have become like family to us. It brings us joy to see you thrive. Please, miss, we mean no harm by it."

Sophia tried to be angry and indignant, but it could not last. It was true—the staff were like her extended family. The various footmen, about whose necks she threw her arms to be carried between rooms. Katie, to whom she had, many a time, owed an easier breath, or the simple comfort of a re-fluffed pillow. Cook, who sent her favorite dishes to her room when she was too exhausted to leave her bed. They knew her, cared for her, in a manner that was beyond mere duty.

Sophia's affront melted away. "I am sure you mean well. Alas, that is my difficulty. Everyone means well. Even Mr. Mannerly." She cast her eyes to the letter once more. "He wants to meet Papa."

"Oh, miss!"

"Exactly. No doubt he thinks it the gentlemanly thing to do. But it is quite impossible. And how should I explain that to him?"

Her voice dropped, sinking with her hopes. "He will discover the madness at the core of this family. And then I will lose him."

She looked up at Katie, tears pooling in her eyes. "Why can't I have this one small thing? Do I ask too much? Just to know such a man exists who admires me as I am? I have kept him at arm's length. I have followed the rules." She balled a fist. "Those infernal rules!"

The tears flowed hotly now.

Katie was across the room in an instant, kneeling beside her. She reached as if to take her mistress's hand to console her, but seemed to think better of it. Instead, she sank to the floor, her upturned face distraught. "Miss Grant... Oh, Miss Grant, don't cry."

But Sophia had held these tears back too long. Now that she had released her emotion, she could not stem its flow.

"I can send for some tea," offered the desperate maid. She sprang up and made for the bell ribbon, but Sophia's shaky voice halted her steps.

"Leave it." She sucked in a deep, tremulous breath. "Tea will not fix what ails me. Nothing can cure that." Her eyes were raw and red, and bitterness crept into her voice. "I must pay the price of my sins."

"Mistress?" Katie stood, her hands helpless at her sides. "Maybe you should speak with the vicar?"

Sophia barked a rough, rueful laugh. "He cannot undo what has been done. No, I must break contact with Mr. Mannerly. This charade must end. I have been the maker of my own calamity. I should face up to its consequences." She stifled a sob. "Even if it breaks my heart."

Katie made to protest, but Sophia shook her head vehemently. "We shall speak no more on this. You have been kindness itself, dear Katie, and I shall not forget it. But I know what I must do. It is pointless to avoid it. Do not press me further."

Katie was the picture of dejection. As if it was *her* world that was collapsing. To her credit, she nodded obediently and took her seat once more, though her eyes were strained as if she, too, had tears to shed. But Sophia had no pity to spare. Her own heart was gutted. And the hardest part still lay before her.

She pulled a sheet of paper closer. It slid easily across the tray. She dipped the quill in ink. It sank and rose in silence, the black liquid coating it gently, like a whisper.

Dear Mr. Mannerly, she wrote in smooth, even strokes, while her heart raged and howled within her. *I thank you for your letter.* No more letters! The pending loss shrieked and clawed at her mind. *As you know, my father is currently away in London for some weeks.* But he would be back. And he would pin her heart to his dreadful collection of imprisoned souls like a butterfly, to be preserved for his enjoyment only. *His return does not, however, signify the possibility of a meeting. To explain this in a letter, to display such words in a permanent form, is not right. Whatever else my father may be, I will not commit his faults to paper.* Faults—her capsizing world remembered, as it tilted into the tumultuous sea of her thoughts—that had been of *her* creation. Oh, Mama! If Papa had only been home that Monday!

If you would be willing to call upon me at ten in the morning, I will make my meaning clear. But I should add—and this will not be debated, sir—that this letter and that meeting will be the last of either. The pain roared through her chest. Her ears filled with a deafening pressure as if drowning.

Thank you for our conversations and all you have contributed to making me a stronger poet. Poetry! Would she ever write another word of it without thinking of him? Her two loves were so intertwined now. Perhaps she had lost them both. The wail of despair soared through her, rising upon a tide that threatened to consume her.

With gratitude, Sophia Grant. She could add nothing more. He would be hurt. He would recover. She could not think of him. She could not stop thinking of him.

She bit hard into the inside of her cheek. She must address the letter before tears ruined her efforts. She did not have it in her to write these words again.

"Katie," she said, the exhaustion shallow in her voice, "have this delivered. And then leave me awhile."

"But, miss…"

"Do as I bid you. There is no harm that can befall me now that could increase the pain I already suffer. I do not wish to be watched while I mourn."

"Yes, miss," Katie answered sadly. She carried the letter from the room, and with it, the finality of Sophia's decision. She closed the door behind her with a soft click. To Sophia, it was the sickening sound of a tomb being sealed. And she was alone within it.

CHAPTER EIGHT

TOBIAS DID NOT lift the brass knocker on the door. There was still time to turn back. He could feign illness, say his uncle needed him, make up an unforeseen emergency. Miss Grant's letter had been so cold, so distant; it was enough to overcome even *his* boundless enthusiasm.

Almost.

In a secret chamber of his heart, he kept the tiniest flame of hope alive. The speed and force with which she had thrown up her defenses were just another manifestation of her insecurity. He was determined to flush it out, once and for all.

Yet he stood and did not knock.

His uncle's warnings rang in his ears. *"Do not push too hard. There is sorrow in this house."* He could not deny the wisdom in being cautious. But time was running out. The situation required drastic measures. He had tried his uncle's way. He had been polite and formal. It had not worked. It had only driven the woman he loved further into herself. For her to abruptly end all correspondence was an extreme action. He would have to match it with his own.

Tobias squared his shoulders. The lovely, brilliant Miss Sophia Grant would be lost to him if his courage failed him. He reached out and, after a brief moment of hesitation, tapped the door with the knocker. It seemed too insignificant a sound to call anyone forth, yet the door swung open, and the butler appeared, his expression predictably neutral, except… Was that a twinkle in his eye?

"Ah, Mr. Mannerly. You are expected." The twinkling butler waved his arm toward the entrance and stepped aside to allow Tobias in. "If you will follow me."

Tobias did so, passing the dining room, where he had already made happy memories. This time, however, they came to a halt outside the drawing room, where the heat of a fire pulsed through the doorway. The door was ajar, and the footman knocked softly.

"Mr. Mannerly is here, Miss Grant."

There was a slightly longer pause than expected. Tobias could imagine Miss Grant's body stiffening with apprehension. Perhaps she was also straightening her skirts, or putting aside her sewing. Eventually, after several seconds that extended unbearably in silence, she said, "Thank you. You may go. I have Katie with me."

The butler nodded to Tobias, twitching away the beginning of a smile, and strode back down the way they had come. A shrewd little face appeared at the door and a hand indicated for him to enter. It was not the elegant hand of Miss Grant, with her long, delicate fingers. There were no dark locks framing handsome features.

As soon as Tobias followed the girl into the room, he spotted Miss Grant on the chaise lounge. His heart soared at the sight of her, all doubts and agitation forgotten. He rushed toward her, his hands extended to grasp hers. He brought the tips of her fingers to his lips and pressed his affection warmly upon them, ignoring the horrified gasp of her lady's maid.

Miss Grant pulled her hands free, wrapping the hand he had kissed inside the other. "Mr. Mannerly," she said, her voice strained, "won't you sit down?"

She was aloof, as she had been in her letter. And yet, her face was flushed, and her eyes were cast shyly away from him. She continued to clasp the hand he had bestowed his tender kiss upon. It did not seem to be the tight clench of regret, but rather a sort of cradling, as if she silently savored the memory of his touch.

He should have been confused. Instead, her inconsistencies gave him confidence that he had read the situation correctly. He had observed this exact behavior repeatedly at dinner two nights before. She had desired him and doubted him, both at once. Of that, he was convinced. When he had asked to meet with her father, she must have guessed what hope filled his heart. And because the poor creature did not think herself worthy, she would not let him try. It was just like her to throw up a barrier to protect herself. If she ended things with him, she could hide herself away once more. If he did not meet her father, he could not ask for her hand. This would be her reasoning.

Well, she was wrong.

Whatever her father's so-called faults might be, Tobias was not discouraged. After all, it was not Mr. Conrad Grant he hoped to marry. He would insist upon the meeting. He would stand his ground. He would show her he was consistent and true. And she would *have* to relent. How could she not if he but loved her enough?

Since he knew she would only try to discourage him, he would not give her the opportunity. He must take the matter by the horns, and do it now.

He gripped the nearest armchair and pulled it up next to the chaise lounge. Miss Grant watched him with the startled expression of someone quite out of her depth. He ignored it and leaned forward, bringing his body even closer, so that she looked at Katie in a mute panic. He gave her no chance to speak. He would not let her protest. Today, no matter how she squirmed under the reality of it, she would know the full measure of his devotion.

"Miss Grant," he began, "thank you for seeing me. I understand full well what you have summoned me to say. But there is something I would have you know." He turned his head toward

Katie. "Might we speak in private?"

Miss Grant shook her head. "That is quite impossible. I am surprised you would ask, sir. I thought you were a man who valued my reputation."

Tobias wanted to kick himself. He had barely said two words, and already he had offended her. He would have to do better, and fast.

"I assure you, my intentions are entirely honorable. But the matter I wish to discuss is…sensitive."

"Mr. Mannerly, Katie is my constant companion. There is nothing that escapes her attention. The theme of our discussion is known to her. She will be discreet."

"It is? She knows why I have come?"

"She does."

"And she will not reveal anything to your father until I have had a chance to present my case to him?"

Miss Grant hesitated. "Sir, I believe I made it clear that there would be no opportunity to speak with my father. This meeting is to be the last. I will give you the necessary insight into my situation that will make you understand. But that will be the end of it."

For a woman so determined in her decision, Tobias observed, she did not appear content with her choice. It was just as he had suspected. She was once more choosing fear over happiness. But he would give her something worth believing in. Whatever she doubted within herself, she must be certain of *him*. It was time to wipe her objections from the table.

"Miss Grant." He spoke a little less boldly than he would have liked, all too aware of the eyes of young Katie boring into the back of his neck. He took a deep breath. "Sophia. You will let me call you 'Sophia'? I cannot unburden my soul to anyone but my dearest Sophia."

"Really, Mr. Mannerly, you…"

"Tobias."

"What?"

"Tobias. Please call me 'Tobias.'"

"I will do no such thing!" Sophia protested. But her ears were quite pink with embarrassed pleasure. And she lifted her hand-cocoon to her breast.

"Sophia, I…"

"*Mr. Mannerly…*"

"Tobias."

"Really, I cannot…"

Tobias sighed. "I have already explained. Regardless of our short acquaintance, we are quite beyond the point of Mr. and Miss. *I* know it. You know it. And what I have to say can bear no further interruption. You may object when I am done."

"Well! That is rather presumptuous, don't you…"

"When I am done, dear Sophia." Tobias laid his finger softly upon his own lips, and Sophia—more from shock than willing-ness—subsided into silence.

"Much of what I would say," he continued, "you already know. At dinner, I expressed my admiration for you at great length. And always you resisted. The reason evades me. I have seen the fondness your family has for you. The low esteem of your own worth therefore originates with you. You have convinced yourself no one could love you—not truly. You have placed the burden of your value upon your weakened legs and lungs. But they have nothing to do with it! You have all the qualities I treasure. You *are* the treasure!"

He stopped to catch his breath, and Sophia immediately opened her mouth to refute all he had said. But Tobias rushed on.

"I know you *want* to believe it. My feelings have been out-spoken and obvious. And I sense that you share them, though you are sensible and restrained in your expression of them. I will not let you drown them out. I know a passionate heart beats in your breast! I have seen it in your writing. I have seen it in your eyes. But you bind your passion tightly with cords of fear. Well, I am here to set it free. I am determined to drive the fear and doubt from your mind. This is no idle declaration. I am committed to you—to us. Marry me, Sophia. Marry me! I give you my heart, my life—unreservedly and forever. Will you give me yours?"

A little gasp of delight percolated up from behind him where Katie sat. But Tobias sought his answer from the woman he loved.

Sophia, far from delighted, froze in place like a deer before the hunter. Then, the cherished kiss no longer cradled, she brought her hands to her mouth to hide the expression of horror stamped upon it.

"It is a shock, I know," Tobias admitted, but Sophia shook her head violently and tears pooled in her eyes.

"How could you?" she whispered.

Of all the responses Tobias had imagined—and he had tried to predict them all—this was not among them.

"I don't understand," he replied honestly.

Sophia wiped her tears roughly and sniffed. "I told myself I knew you. I believed you were a man of honor. And yet you mock me."

"Mock you? *Mock* you?" Tobias spluttered. "I offer you everything I have, and you think I mock you? How, pray, have you come to such a monstrous conclusion?"

She stared at him accusingly, her mouth tight with bitterness. "You say you love me, but you are lying to yourself. You have spent but a few hours in my company. You have not been here when I struggle to catch my breath. You have not seen my withered legs. I am a grotesque version of womanhood. You have not seen enough to understand that. You have no business offering me romance when my daily reality would spoil it all."

"Sophia," Tobias almost pleaded, "I don't care about these things. What need have I of a wife with a robust body when we can spend our days poring over the works of great authors, yourself included? Why would I go riding with a woman who is silly or churlish or demanding when I could sit in the company of one whose character and intellect inspires me? Notwithstanding your own opinion, I find you exquisite in every way."

"You don't mean that!" Sophia cried, a stifled sob escaping.

"Yes, I do! I know I am bungling this, but you forced my hand. I would have been more patient, given you time to come to these conclusions yourself. But you threatened to cut me off entirely! What was I to do but declare myself at once? I cannot lose you, dearest Sophia. Punish me for my impertinence. Scold me each time we meet. But never, never tell my heart it does not know what it feels. I love you, Sophia. You must accept that. Tell your fears they have had their turn. Now it is time to embrace life. There is no better fit for me than you. Let me make you happy."

Sophia burst into a flood of tears.

Tobias could stand it no longer. He leaped from his chair and wrapped her in his arms. He gently cupped her face against his shoulder while she wept, strands of her damp hair clinging to his cheek. "There, my love, all is well. You are safe."

At these words, Sophia pulled herself abruptly from his embrace. "*You* are not," she hiccup-sobbed. "I c-cannot h-h-have you s-sacrifice yourself for me."

"Oh, you precious fool, it is no sacrifice." He smiled and wiped away her tears with his thumbs. "You are the greatest gift."

"No! I am a curse!" She thrust his hand from her. "You must not align your life with mine. I will ruin it."

Tobias took hold of her wrists and drew her toward him. "Enough of this. Look at me. *Look at me.* What are you so afraid of? Surely, you cannot still doubt me? What more must I do to prove I will not fail you?"

Sophia's eyes fixed upon his, wild and frightened. "I am not afraid of you, Tobias. I am afraid of *me*. You mustn't love me. I will drag you to your doom."

And with that, she buried her face in her hands and wept once more.

Tobias was utterly perplexed. Something was at work here he could not fathom. This was much more than insecurity. Sophia was absolutely terrified.

He turned helplessly to Katie. A worried frown pleated her brow. He wished he could ask her what to do, but that would not be proper. Katie must have felt the same, for she tilted her head toward her mistress and silently mouthed, *Help her!*

If only he knew how!

At a loss, he sat mute and fretting while Sophia emptied herself of emotion long suppressed. When she subsided to the occasional sniffle, Tobias did the only thing he could think of—he offered her his handkerchief. She blew her nose—an earthy, wholesome sound that broke some of the tension in the room.

Sophia looked at the damp cloth apologetically. "I am sorry. I have made a terrible scene."

"You do not need to apologize. You have done nothing wrong. But perhaps you could explain? There is something at the heart of the matter that you have not told me. It would help if I understood."

Sophia gave a shuddering sigh. "I can see there is no other way. You will not release me until you grasp the danger you are in."

"Danger? Tell me."

Sophia twisted the corner of the handkerchief until it was tightly coiled. She licked her lips to moisten them. A deep breath followed. And another. Finally, she lifted her head to Tobias. "When I am done, you must go. It will be too painful to see the revulsion on your face. You will do me this one kindness."

"I cannot imagine anything that would cause…"

"Promise me!"

"We shall see."

Sophia hesitated. Her eyes flicked toward Katie, then back to Tobias. She clenched her fingers and inhaled slowly one more time. "Very well. But I wish you could have spared me this."

A pang of guilt—for what, he did not yet know—pinched at his conscience. All he could hope for was that the discovery of the truth would erase all the suffering it had caused.

"When I was fourteen," Sophia explained, "I had the paralysis fever. We did not know it at first. It is not so common an ailment as influenza or other fevers. As with any other childhood illness, my father kept me isolated with a maid and a nurse to tend to me. But I grew weaker, and my symptoms frightened me."

She shivered, wrapping her arms around herself as if to fend off the memory.

"My breathing grew labored and my legs too heavy to move. I was certain I was dying. I was convinced I would succumb to this strange illness with no one by my side except those paid to be there. I begged the nurse to fetch my mother. But my father had given strict orders. And the nurse obeyed."

Her narration stopped. Sophia was struggling against new tears, and her lips twitched as she fought to quash them. She swallowed hard.

"Every Monday," she continued haltingly, "Papa...he always... It is the day he deals with business away from home. This day was no different. He left the house...left me as I was at death's door. I confess that in that moment I hated him. I was afraid, and I was angry. I no longer cared what he thought or did. I only knew that, if I were to leave this world, I wanted my mother to see me across that threshold. And his absence gave me that one chance."

Sophia began to rock, a futile attempt to soothe herself.

"I pleaded once more with the nurse, convinced her that Papa need never know, and that I deserved to have my mother with me as I took my last breath." A soft moan escaped her throat.

"Of course my mother came. What mother would refuse such a petition? She held my hand for hours. And though she grew fatigued, she wiped my brow and coaxed me to take a sip of broth. Her presence gave me strength. I did not die."

Sophia raised her dolorous gaze to Tobias.

"Every day after that, I grew stronger. My fever abated. My breathing improved." She shivered with apprehension as she prepared to utter words that seemed to have haunted her for years. "But in her room, attended only by a maid and a nurse, my mother sickened. You see," she said bitterly, "my father had been harsh, but he was right. I had been a danger to the family. In my selfishness, I had made my mother ill."

She looked at her hands. Tobias wondered what solace she hoped they might offer. Certainly, she spoke to them as if they did. "Three weeks after she had tended to my needs," she murmured, "my mother died alone."

Sophia grew very still, silenced, perhaps, by the weight of the memory bearing down on her.

Tobias sensed her helplessness and shared in it. He had no words. What was there he could say to undo such great sorrow?

But Sophia was not done. She looked at Tobias, her body sagging with a weariness and resignation that was half a lifetime in the making. Her voice was dull, all her energy and courage spent.

"Now, Mr. Mannerly, you will do me the courtesy of leaving my terrible secret behind when you go. I have told you so that you may understand. And if you are half the man that I believe you are, you would not shame me by repeating any of it."

The very idea was repugnant to Tobias. "To break your trust thus would be unthinkable! I can only imagine the pain you have suffered to lose your mother at such a tender age, and to do so without a proper goodbye..."

Sophia's face twisted into a scowl. "You think *that* is my greatest burden? Do you understand nothing? I *killed* her! In my selfishness, I made demands, and she died for it!" An edge of hysteria touched her speech.

"You were but a child!" Tobias exclaimed. "If your father had not kept you apart, I have no doubt she would have been by your side every day. The fever caused her death, Sophia, not you."

"No! Do not try to make excuses for me. It was me, my illness, that ended her life. I would have recovered without her visit, and she would still be alive today."

"You don't know that. She may have suffered a different disease in a subsequent year. If the tables had been turned, and she had made you ill, would you have thrust such guilt upon her? Would you have wanted her to throw away her life and her chance at happiness because the fates had been unkind?"

"It wasn't fate," Sophia insisted. "There was nothing random about it. It was I, and I alone, who went against my father's wishes and made demands because I was a coward. I robbed my father, sisters, brothers of a wife and mother."

"A coward? You truly believe that? You think your mother did not desperately want to enter that room? She just needed an excuse. She would never, ever have let you die alone. Even if your father had been home, if she'd known you were close to death, not all the bars and bolts in the world could have locked her out of that room. Your father would not have stood a chance against a mother's love."

"But I wasn't dying after all! I was just afraid." She pressed her palms to her face, dragging them slowly down to her mouth, which opened to a shuddering breath. "If I had been braver, she would have stayed away, as my father wished."

"Sophia." Tobias softened his voice. "You were very ill. I suspect your mother knew that. That was why she came. Her comforting presence is what saved you. It gave you the will to fight. She knew the risk. She made the sacrifice willingly. It was her choice. You did nothing wrong."

Sophia stared at him as if seeing him for the first time. "You think she knew?"

"I am certain of it."

"She would have come anyway, even if I had said nothing?"

"If you were as ill as you say, I don't doubt it for a second."

"I… I …" She choked back the relief. "I am not wicked?"

"No, my darling, far from it."

"I won't hurt you too?" Her eyes were filled with a hopeful pleading.

Tobias smiled. "Oh, you will hurt me, in a human sort of way. But I will scold you a little and then forgive you."

"You won't…die?" Her words were barely audible, as if uttering them might make the threat more real.

"We all must die, dearest one. But you are no grim reaper. I am quite safe with you." He gave a wry smile. "Of course, you do torture my poor heart most cruelly. Fortunately, there is an easy remedy for that."

"What is it?" she asked shyly.

"Say *yes*."

"Yes?"

"Yes. Yes to being my wife. Yes to living life more fully. Yes to everything that fear and guilt has robbed you of until now."

"Oh."

"Is that not what you want? Beneath all those layers of self-imposed blame, have you not desired the contentment of love well met?"

"Of course I have desired it. But I have never given myself permission to reach for it."

"You will now, won't you?" Tobias coaxed gently.

"I... I'm not... It will take time. I am not yet used to the idea that I may ask for such happiness."

"Do you at least acknowledge now that you may?"

Sophia hesitated. Fifteen years of repression and denial would be hard to shake off. "I... I think so."

"Say it. Say, 'I deserve to be loved.'"

"I'm not sure..."

"Then let us *make* it a certainty. Say it, and believe it."

"I...deserve..." Sophia swallowed, the effort of saying words she had so long rejected driving a flush into her cheeks.

"You can do it."

"I deserve...to...be...loved." She rushed the last word, then beamed at Tobias in triumph.

"Again."

"I deserve to be loved." Her smile broadened.

"Yes, dearest! How right you are!" Tobias clasped her hands in his and drew them to his lips.

Sophia did not resist.

Joy, oh, joy! To behold his beloved surfacing from the gloom of her past was enough to lift all the confusion and frustration Tobias had felt until now. He was but one word away from making her his wife, one word from becoming the happiest man alive. One little "yes" and they would be able to start their life together. So close.

And yet.

Sophia was fragile, teetering on the edge of a new dawn, her future suddenly thrown open before her. He must not push. Not now. All was new and brittle. He must not force the fledgling from its nest. If ever he was going to exercise wisdom and restraint, this was the most critical moment.

"Sophia," he said, bringing her hands toward his heart.

"Hmm?" she murmured dreamily.

"Would you permit me to call upon you again? As often as you are comfortable. We can discuss your poetry. Or the weather. And, when you are ready, we might revisit our talk of the future. Our future."

"Yes." The corner of her mouth dimpled into a smile. "I would like that. To meet again, I mean." Her eyes flicked away abruptly. "As for the rest, you must bear with me. I cannot yet grasp such big hopes." There was a pause, and then her gaze lifted to his once more. "There is much for me to think about. It is strange to view my life, my past, through a different lens."

Inside, Tobias's heart did somersaults of excitement. On the surface, he took great pains to hold back. He pressed her hands to his lips once more, then returned them to her lap. "Whenever you are ready, I will be here." Oh, how hard it was to resist her! To release her when he wished to pull her closer. To wait. To let her lead. His whole body vibrated internally with anticipation. When would she speak?

"Mondays." Sophia gulped. "Papa is away every Monday."

"I am not afraid to meet your father."

"I am not ready."

Tobias bit his lip. One thing at a time. He had promised.

"Very well," he said, "Mondays it is. Together, we shall make new, happier memories for this day."

Relief washed over Sophia's entire being. "That would be welcome...Tobias."

She blushed—not the mortified flush of embarrassment she had worn so often before, but the warm tinge of a woman touched unexpectedly by happiness and love.

The glow of it enveloped Tobias. Everything tingled and buzzed. He wanted to jump up and dance a jig, fling the door open, and shout to the world that he was the luckiest man alive.

Instead, he reached into his coat pocket and drew out a small book. "I have brought this volume of poetry by an outstanding poet of our time." He passed the book to Sophia. "I was hoping she might sign it for me."

Sophia sat up a little straighter and beckoned to Katie to bring her writing tray. "To whom shall I address it?" she asked with mock curiosity.

"I shall leave that for you to decide," Tobias answered.

Sophia smiled broadly. She took up her quill at once and, having inked it, wrote with a careful hand while speaking the words aloud. "To dear Tobias." She paused, turned a charming shade of pink, and continued, "...my beloved." *Scribble, scribble.* "The author of my happiness."

She signed it with a flourish, blotted it with care, then passed the book back to Tobias, their fingers brushing and lingering for a long moment.

Tobias cleared his throat. "Actually, there is a passage you wrote..." He paged through the book to find it. "Ah, here it is. I was hoping you could elucidate your choice of metaphor in this stanza."

"Let me see," said Sophia, reaching for the small volume once more.

Instead, Tobias closed the book with his finger as place-keeper, took hold of the armrest of his chair, and turned it about so that he was no longer facing Sophia, but almost side by side with her. He opened to the page and leaned in so that they might read the contents together.

Sophia tilted her head down, her hair falling forward and obscuring her face. Tenderly, Tobias caught her curls with his fingertips and drew them back, his touch tracing a line of electric pleasure across her cheek. The heat rushed to her exposed neck. Her scent permeated his giddy mind.

She leaned her cheek against the back of his fingers and closed her eyes. One slow breath and she had opened her lips to his hand. Her warm, moist breath roused his desire to a furnace. Tobias could be cautious no more. In a moment, his mouth was upon hers, his hands seeking her waist, pulling her in, closing the space between them. He felt her body stiffen, then relax, as she answered his yearning with her own.

The ink tray hit the floor with a thud and clatter. They jumped back in shock. Katie sprang up to clear the mess.

Katie. Tobias had quite forgotten about her.

"Oh, dear," said Sophia, clearly trying to regain her composure, "we have made quite a mess. I'm sorry, Katie."

Katie grinned. "That's all right, miss. I'll have it cleaned up in no time." She looked away as her grin widened. "I'll have to fetch some warm water and a cloth to remove the ink from the carpet. I will be away a few minutes—if that's all right with you, miss?"

A coy smile told him it was perfectly all right with Sophia. As the door closed behind the still-smiling maid, Tobias scooped his beloved up in his arms once more. Until a firm knock should draw them reluctantly apart, he would show her that it was more than all right with him too.

CHAPTER NINE

IT WAS TUESDAY. Sophia had watched the snow fall all day Monday and cursed it. She had had the entire weekend to ponder Tobias's words. His touch. And now, his absence.

Why had she told him to return only on Mondays? Father was away for weeks yet. Every day was available to them. And, now that she had begun to come to terms with her past, she wanted her present to be filled with Tobias. She did not know how long this bond they had would last. She would grasp whatever she could with both hands. Sophia felt a recklessness return. As if she were once again a girl with her whole life ahead of her. For as long as possible, she wanted Tobias to be a part of it.

Then it had snowed. All. Day. Long.

Typically, she would have resigned herself to a week of waiting, longsuffering being one of the few qualities her narrow world had endorsed. But not today. This morning, when the fresh snow glittered under a clear blue sky, she had written to Tobias.

He would come. She knew he would. Nothing could possibly...

THUD!

Sophia whipped her head around. A splatter of snow clung to the window pane.

Katie had already jumped up and run toward it when another

thud and a spray of snow against the glass caused her to duck instinctively. She straightened up cautiously and peered outside. A cry of delight erupted and she turned to her mistress, her voice filled with laughter.

"It's Mr. Mannerly!"

Sophia's heart beat faster at once.

"Go and fetch him. Tell him to come inside." She had already begun to straighten her skirts.

A different sort of thudding emanated from the passage as heavy boots approached. George appeared around the door. His long, black hair—unlike their father's perfectly manicured look—hung about his face in wild abandon. Sophia wondered if he still occasionally chewed on the ends, as he had done as a boy.

"I say!" he declared. "Your chap gave me quite the start! I was in my room upstairs and botched a letter I was writing. I shall have to begin again." He held up a hand almost as slender as her own, a smear of ink on the tips of his thumb and forefinger.

"Sorry, George. Tobias meant no harm."

"Of course not," her brother answered good-naturedly. "Still, he deserves to be punished. Especially if we have moved on to the familiarity of first names already." He patted his pockets in an absentminded way. "I wonder where my gloves are?"

Sophia's eyes widened. "What are you going to do?"

"Well, I clearly can't get back to my duties until I have shown your young fellow how to throw a snowball properly." George winked. "Let's see if he can hit a moving target."

"Ooo! Can I come too?" squealed a voice behind him. George stepped to the side and revealed young Bess, who was clapping her hands, her plump cheeks glowing with anticipation.

"I don't see why not," George replied. "In fact, let's collect Henry and Adriana to help us man the battle stations."

"Hey, that's not fair!" exclaimed Sophia. "You can't just run off and have fun with Tobias while I'm stuck here in this room. He came to see *me*, after all."

George hesitated. "I'm certain he will spend several hours

with you, Fee. Just give us twenty minutes."

Sophia folded her arms. "Absolutely not! You're taking me with you."

Her brother's expression grew serious. "Come on, Fee, you know we can't do that. Father would have our hides."

"He's not here now," Sophia retorted stubbornly. "Besides, if you can keep it secret that Tobias came to visit, a snowball fight should be no different."

"But it is. This could make you ill."

"George, what is the point of being alive if I'm not actually living?"

Her brother was silent.

"I promise to bundle up warmly."

No answer.

"If you don't do this, I shall tell Papa you let me go out in the carriage when it was snowing."

George's mouth flew open. "You little horror! I'd forgotten what an absolute tyrant you could be. I see it hasn't taken you long to return to old habits."

Sophia grinned triumphantly. "Shall I call a footman, or will you do the honors?"

"I'll send for a footman," George grumbled. "But *you* will sit upon a chair and keep a rug under your feet."

"Of course," Sophia answered meekly. "Whatever you say."

Her brother gave her a look that suggested he wasn't fooled for a second. "I have a feeling we haven't seen the last of your mischief, Fee. Do be gentle with us. We are out of practice, old girl."

Sophia sucked in her breath in pretended indignation. "You will pay for that, George! *Old girl*, indeed! I shall hurl my first snowball at your swollen head."

"I'm not afraid. You throw like a girl." George laughed over his shoulder as he strode out of the room.

OUTSIDE, TOBIAS GATHERED Sophia to himself the moment the footman lowered her feet to the ground. She clung to him rather more than she needed to, waiting for the chair to be brought for her at George's insistence.

"You certainly know how to make an entrance," she whispered into his warm neck as she nuzzled closer.

"As do you. I had not expected to have you join me in this chill. It is safe for you, I hope? You do not take unnecessary risks?" He stroked her flushed cheeks with the back of his fingers.

"On the contrary. It will do me the world of good. I can't remember when last I have played outside with my family."

Tobias looked up at Adriana, who was rapidly building a mound of snowballs for her arsenal. "I suspect it will be a fearsome battle. Should you not watch from a distance?'

"No, the general should lead the charge."

"I see." The corner of his mouth lifted in a lopsided grin. "I am to be conscripted into your service."

"You object?"

"Oh, no, I am more than willing to die for you."

Sophia's smile vanished. "I need no sacrifice of that nature," she said stiffly.

Tobias rapped his knuckles against his forehead. "I am such a dolt! I chose those words very poorly indeed." His hand returned to hers. "Forgive me, Dearest. I have spoken my thoughts before they are well formed. It remains a fault I seem unable to master." His head hung low with shame.

The comment still smarted. Still, Sophia was willing to let it go. He had meant nothing by it. It belonged with sorrows of the past. Best they were *left* in the past. Besides, Adriana was already building a wall of snow for her defenses. There was no time to waste.

"Come on," she directed as she lowered herself onto the seat the footman had just delivered. "We shall catch them off guard. Adriana first. Her eyes are not upon the enemy."

Tobias grabbed fistfuls of snow and formed them quickly with his gloved hands, a small pile of ammunition accumulating beside the chair, within Sophia's reach. With several more stacked in his palm, he took a stand. Lifting his knee, he raised his arm up, elbow retracted, then released his first volley at Adriana's unsuspecting back.

She shrieked with surprise and spun around to identify her attacker. "Oh, so it's to be war with the Mannerlys. To me, Grants! Defend the family honor!"

A barrage of snowy projectiles launched from all directions. Tobias twisted around and planted his body in front of Sophia, shielding her from the worst of it. A cascade of snow slid from his coat.

"Step aside, quickly!" yelled the ungrateful Sophia. As he did so, she threw a single shot at stocky, little Bess, who was nearest, and whose billowing cloak made her an easy target. The weak attempt was nevertheless successful and Sophia laughed breathlessly as the rest of her siblings renewed their attack.

Once again, Tobias absorbed the onslaught, his face stoic, his eyes fixed upon his precious charge. *Thump, thump, thump.* The snowballs landed on his back, one knocking his hat from his head. His rumpled curls fell free and, for a moment, Sophia forgot the battle. She gazed at the handsome man before her, his blue eyes determined, his collar filled with snow, which melted down his warm neck, his messy hair calling for the touch of her fingers.

More snow hit her valiant protector.

"Mercy!" Sophia cried. "It is four against two. And our general is incapacitated. We need reinforcements." She coughed a little as she said this.

There was an abrupt ceasefire.

George crossed the battlefield. "We yield. It is time to go indoors."

"But we have barely begun," complained Sophia.

"And already it affects you," George replied sternly.

"I am perfectly fine." Sophia sulked, trying to suppress a cough and failing.

"Then take pity on poor Mr. Mannerly, who has had the worst of it. He needs a warm fire and a cup of hot cocoa as much as you do." He beckoned to the footman before she could protest further.

Sophia looked upon her brave soldier—his coat wet with melting snow, his hair starting to drip—and relented.

"I release you from your commission," she declared. "You will accompany me to the barracks for sustenance and"—she offered him a most particular tilt of the head—"further reward."

"Hmm," George added dryly, "I shall have Katie tend upon you. Just to make sure the fire is not too hot."

"Yes." Adriana smirked as she trudged past them in the snow. "We wouldn't want the *fire* to get too hot."

"I don't understand," Bess inquired as she took Adriana's arm. "Sophia has always *liked* the fire to be hot. Father complains she uses up the coal faster than any of us."

Adriana patted her little sister's hand. "You are right. As ladies get older, they prefer a, *ahem*, warmer fire. Give it time. You will see. However, it's always best to avoid the dangers of too *much* heat. Isn't that so, George?"

George and Henry looked straight ahead with great determination as they marched back to the house, although Sophia was certain Henry stifled a brief snort. Then a footman lifted her lightly into the air. She threw her arms around the man's shoulders, wishing it could be Tobias who carried her off instead.

The truth was, she knew he never could. But that was a problem for another day.

CHAPTER TEN

"WE SHALL BE having a guest for dinner this evening."

Lord Carthige's announcement was so unlikely, it took Tobias a few moments to find his tongue.

"Did you hear me, Nephew?"

"*Why?*" Tobias marveled. "I mean, who?"

"Viscount Howell." Lord Carthige said coolly, as if it were nothing of consequence.

"*The* Lord Howell? Here?" Tobias was flummoxed. Uncle Edmund didn't even visit with his neighbors. Now they were about to receive the most powerful man in their great northern city.

"His father and I were acquainted."

"'Were'?"

"He died some months ago." His uncle shrugged. "Sad, but not tragic. He was a… difficult man." Lord Carthige picked at the knee of his trousers. Then he folded his hands and looked up. "The new viscount is a creature of greater depth."

Tobias smiled to himself. Only his uncle would use the word "creature" to describe a fellow human being, especially one he seemed to like.

"What is the occasion?" Tobias asked, still trying to make sense of his uncle's sudden willingness to accommodate company.

"There is none. He has requested a meeting, and I suggested dinner. I feel sorry for the lad. He is quite alone in the world now."

"Has he no family at all?"

"Oh, no, there is a mother and two sisters. But they are no comfort to him. And the burden of responsibility he must now shoulder is great indeed. I would take him under my wing, as I have done you." Uncle Edmund cast his eyes upon Tobias and added, "He reminds me a little of you, now that I think of it."

"I cannot imagine what a man in such an unenviable position has in common with myself," mused Tobias.

Edmund shrugged. "You are of a similar age, well educated, confident in your expertise, and equally hapless around women."

"I see," Tobias answered, though in truth, he did not see at all. Had he not won the heart of his true love? That should count for something, even if matters had not gone equally as smoothly with Miss Mary Dunbar. Besides, his uncle was not one to judge. He had chosen a life of solitude over marriage. "Perhaps you underestimate him," he suggested.

"You will see," was all the answer Tobias received.

THE SUN WAS setting when the carriage with the Howell crest pulled up on the drive. Tobias had stationed himself at a front-facing window. It was not very gentlemanly to spy on one's guest, but Tobias could not help himself. Nothing much happened at Newcliffe Hall except reading and cataloguing. The newcomer was a curiosity, and Tobias was undeniably curious.

A tall, broad-shouldered man descended the carriage steps. The manner in which he carried himself matched his physique. This, along with his straight nose and dark, brooding looks would no doubt appeal to the fairer sex if he had not already carried a title with which to attract them. Tobias could imagine swaths of ladies swooning at his feet. He certainly could not picture a scenario in which his lordship would appear "hapless," despite what his uncle had said.

Tobias hurried back along the corridor to hear Uncle Edmund say, "Has it been a year already? Well, well, I have been a bad friend. You were right to seek me out. I shall make amends forthwith."

Both host and guest swiveled at the sound of Tobias's arrival.

"Ah, Tobias, just in time. Howell, may I introduce my nephew, Mr. Mannerly? Tobias, this is Lord Howell, our guest."

The viscount extended his hand and took Tobias's in a firm grip. There was just enough to it for its owner to express his authority, yet not so much as to be intimidating. It was a good handshake, and Tobias returned it with equal honesty.

"I was pleased to hear Lord Carthige had acquired your assistance," the viscount said with a surprising degree of warmth. "He does lonely work. No doubt you are good for him."

"You shan't steal him from me, Howell," Uncle Edmund warned, though his voice held no real threat.

"No, indeed, nor could he fulfill the role where I need someone the most."

"Oh?"

To Tobias's complete astonishment, the viscount blushed. All semblance of power and control disintegrated upon the pink-cheeked face.

"Yes, well, erm… That is, in part, why I have sought you out, Carthige. I am in desperate need of solid advice."

"I would be only too happy to help, if I can." He extended an arm, open-palmed, tilting his head toward its length. "Shall we make our way to the dining room? I find it easier to ponder weighty matters on a full stomach."

Tobias followed the other two men and waited his turn to be seated. His uncle nodded to the butler, who indicated the soup tureen to the footman in attendance.

Tobias groaned inwardly. There was always soup. He wished

he did not have to negotiate with a soup spoon in front of the viscount. He arranged his napkin carefully, hoping it would capture any errant drops he might fail to maneuver safely to his lips.

"I wonder that there should be any matter you are not prepared for," his uncle said to their guest, cutting to the heart of the visit, all niceties of conversation bypassed.

It did not seem to bother the viscount. Rather, the gentleman appeared grateful to get his awkward mission over and done with.

"Certainly," he agreed, "my father gave me ample training for the varied roles my position demands. And, until recently, Mother has run the household. Even now that she has chosen to live with Georgina—where her three grandsons are—the house runs smoothly largely out of habit."

"It seems you have it all in hand. I cannot imagine where my help is needed."

"Ah." The blush returned to the viscount's cheeks. "Yes. If it were up to me, I would consider the problem irrelevant. But, as you know yourself, Carthige, there is the expectation of..." He cleared his throat. "Yes, well...of an heir." His eyes fixed on his folded napkin, which his fingers harassed with a degree of vexation.

Uncle Edmund leaned back in his chair. "I see." He exhaled loudly. "That path does not always run smoothly." There was a heaviness to his voice. The sound of...regret?

Tobias had never asked why his uncle was not married. He had just assumed it was not in his nature. Not all men were suited to wedded life. It seemed the same problem plagued the viscount. As far as he could tell, Uncle Edmund had far more in common with the viscount than he did. They were both learned men who enjoyed their own company best. Perhaps it was wiser for it to remain that way.

"Pardon me, my lord," Tobias interjected, "but does your letter patent not allow for one of your nephews to inherit the title? It would appear you have them in ample supply."

Lord Howell gave Tobias a pointed look. "You cannot be blamed for viewing that as a solution. It is not. Even if such an exception to the rules of inheritance were applied, I would not rely upon it. You have not met my sisters. They will not raise the sort of gentlemen who would make fine leaders."

Uncle Edmund looked with sadness upon his friend. "Your sense of duty is admirable, dear boy. However, it may be a steep price to pay—giving up the little personal freedom you have—if your bride is no better than Georgina or Vivienne."

"You have put your finger upon the very reason I am here." Lord Howell leaned forward in his chair. "Where am I to find a worthy woman? Goodness knows she is not among my peers. For a city so large, Munro has produced very few ladies of quality. Those who exist have been claimed, and rightly so. What is left, I fear, is a slurry of silly, spoiled women, several of them quite unpleasant too. What do I have but a selection of tittering foolishness or nasty sirens in satin and lace? It is enough to make my skin crawl."

Tobias flashed a sideways glance at his uncle, but it was not returned. Miss Mary Dunbar was not on his uncle's mind.

"Must she be a nobleman's daughter?" Uncle Edmund asked. "You might have better luck among the gentry."

Lord Howell sighed a deep, protracted sigh. "They move too much in the same circles. These gentlewomen—if such a term could be applied to them—are proud, without deserving to be. You know how rare a kind heart and good nature are, Carthige."

Uncle Edmund was quiet. Tobias sensed that his thoughts were far away. Perhaps his uncle had once yearned for love and had stumbled against the same barrier as the viscount now did. How blessed Tobias felt to have found Sophia! He wished such fulfillment for all good souls.

"If I may," he ventured a suggestion. "You could consider a young lady from the country. Here, where the church bells of Munro ring only on the edge of hearing, we are less under the influence of the city's jaded ways. I can vouch for a better class of person among our country cousins."

Lord Howell perked up a little. "I take it you have met with some success of your own."

"He has set his cap at Miss Sophia Grant," Uncle Edmund confirmed.

"The name is familiar…" The viscount furrowed his brow in thought.

"She is a published poet of unparalleled skill." Tobias beamed, his chest swelling with pride.

"Ah, yes. Now that I think of it, I have come across a small volume of her works. She has an excellent grasp of the human condition. And yet there is a strong note of the classics."

"Miss Grant is fluent in Latin and Greek," Tobias boasted, as if they were his own achievements. "And she corresponds with the likes of Lord Byron, Mr. Wordsworth, and several notable academics."

Lord Howell nodded. "You are well matched, by the sound of it. You have been most fortunate."

"Not as fortunate as you might think," Uncle Edmund countered. "Her father is Mr. Conrad Grant, my neighbor."

Lord Howell sucked the air in between his teeth. "That does complicate things." He looked at Tobias with pity. "I had not realized. I am so sorry."

"I do not fear Mr. Grant." Tobias stuck his chin out. "He will soon see the difference in his daughter now that she has been freed of her past. When he returns from London, it will be a time of celebration, I think."

Uncle Edmund and Lord Howell exchanged glances.

"What?" Tobias asked. "You do not believe me?"

"Oh, it is clear you are devoted to Miss Grant," the viscount answered. "And there is little doubt she is the better for it. But Mr. Grant might cling to the past a little more…insistently."

Tobias opened his mouth with a ready retort, then snapped it shut again. There was no point in trying to persuade the duo of hopeless bachelors of the merits of true love. They had not seen the change in Sophia. But her father would see it. It would gladden his heart. In no time at all, their families would be united in love and matrimony.

He remained less communicative for the remainder of the evening. The pleasantness of having company had been marred by his companions' persistent pessimism. He listened as they debated the merits of families farther from Munro. Uncle Edmund offered to write to his sister and discover the chatter surrounding the season's debutants. A woman's perspective would be useful, and Tobias's mother was sensible to boot. She might even be willing to reach out to her friends in other counties to hear if any hidden gems were waiting to be discovered.

Tobias listened, yes, and wondered at the chance of success of such an arrangement among strangers. He counted himself lucky indeed to have found his beloved almost on his doorstep. Tomorrow, he would visit again. And the day after that. And, in a few short months, he would ask Mr. Grant for her hand.

Uncle Edmund might have his books, and Lord Howell might one day have his heir, but he, Tobias Mannerly, would have the happy ending.

CHAPTER ELEVEN

HOW WAS IT possible—Sophia pondered, as the carriage rattled along the country road—that in the short space of a month, she had completely shrugged off her morbid apprehension of Mondays? Even with Papa back home, she had recovered quickly from his restrictive presence, shoving aside the influence he would normally exert over her mood. After all, come each Monday, he would be away, and the day would be filled with promise.

She glanced at Tobias beside her, his warm hand holding hers. He was peering through the window at the meadow, which was awakening to its first flowers. Sophia knew if he should turn to her, the buds of spring would be forgotten. His gaze would consume her. Just the thought of it made the heat rise to her breast. She scarcely felt the April chill.

She had missed this—seeing nature stir from its sleep. She felt as if she were doing the same, drifting into consciousness after a long absence from the world. Father had forbidden her to leave the house, except in high summer, when he believed the risk to her health was minimal. In some ways, however, summer was too rich for her blood. Its sumptuous beauty and lushness contrasted too starkly with her own existence. The sudden opulence overloaded her senses.

Spring was shy and quieter. Not all birds had returned from

their annual journey, and their song was less overwhelming. Green tips hinted at new growth. It was, as seasons go, more subtle. This was something a poet could appreciate.

Like the spring, Sophia felt a new vitality. Her heart was sending its roots deep into fertile soil. Her mind explored new possibilities. Even her limbs grew a little stronger, as if they were inspired to keep up with the rest of her. The more she threw off the shackles of her past, the easier it was to reach for her dreams.

She curled her fingers tighter around Tobias's. His head swung toward her. And there it was...that look. Her toes wriggled with pleasure inside her soft, leather boots. She no longer blushed. Well, not much, anyway. She was becoming used to the consistency of Tobias's affection. He never wavered in his devotion to her. Gradually, she was allowing herself to simply enjoy it.

He drew her hand to his lips, pressing their soft warmth against the inside of her wrist. The rush of heat surged up her arm. She leaned more tightly against his powerful chest. His embrace enveloped her, his breath in her ear. Exhilaration thrilled through Sophia, a tremor of delight. She felt both safe and reckless.

Tobias uttered a low groan and pulled back.

"You are almost home," he said, his voice husky with re-strained desire.

The carriage wheels made a familiar grinding sound as their muddy rims picked up bits of gravel from the drive leading up to the house. Sophia tucked her curls in place. Assuming a prim posture, she waited for the steps to be lowered, casting her gaze across the drive.

Adriana was standing at the top of the entrance stairs, wearing her warmest coat. She was likely waiting to take the carriage into town.

A movement just inside the doorway caught Sophia's eye. She recognized Freddy Wynn at once. No doubt he was also taking advantage of Papa's absence. But a moment later, her sister hurriedly shooed him back into the shadowy recess of the entrance.

That was odd.

Adriana smiled and waved as the carriage approached, but her eyes flicked back to Freddy with nervous energy. She clutched her skirts, even though no wind tugged at them. As the carriage drew closer, Sophia could just make out a large, dark object jutting out from behind one of the stout pillars.

It was Mama's travel chest.

Sophia's stomach lurched. Her heart pounded painfully against her ribs as the footman fumbled with the folding steps. The moment he stepped back, she threw herself out of the carriage and took the stairs two at a time, stumbling into Adriana's arms when her legs gave out.

"What is happening?" Sophia managed to say between ragged breaths.

"It is time, Fee."

"Time? For what?"

But she knew the answer.

"I'm leaving, Fee. Freddy and I are getting married."

Sophia fought against the suffocating pressure on her chest. "You're abandoning me?"

"No! I'm leaving you in the capable hands of Mr. Mannerly here." Adriana offered Tobias a warm smile. "You will take care of her for me, won't you?"

"You can't go!" Sophia gasped. "Not like this. Papa will never forgive you!"

Adriana's mouth tightened. "Papa offers me no alternative."

"He will banish you from the house! I will never see you again!"

"We will write each other. Katie will make sure you get my letters."

Sophia's voice shrunk to a whisper. "Please don't do this. Please."

"I'm sorry, Fee. You know I would do almost anything for

you. That's why Freddy and I have waited this long. I wanted to make sure you had a future of your own. Now that you have found happiness, you must surely understand why I cannot give Freddy up."

A tear slipped down Sophia's cheek. Tobias leaned in and gently wiped it away with his handkerchief. His face was clouded with concern, the usual ease replaced with drawn brows and lips pressed firmly together.

Freddy stepped forward and put his arm around Adriana, who offered him a weak smile. Only then did Sophia allow herself to see the pain in her sister's eyes.

"We are family," Sophia murmured. "A wedding should be a day of celebration. Our neighbors should be there." She stopped. "I suppose you didn't call the banns."

"No. We didn't dare. Even though Father was away, someone would have told him. But that's all right." She tilted a smile at Freddy. "I am of age. We will simply marry under common license. Freddy has arranged everything. His parents have permitted us the use of the cottage at their summer home. They are waiting there to receive us with a modest celebration. It is barely an hour away and Freddy will have a position with a friend of his father's. We will have an income and the support of the Wynns. You will see. All will be well."

"But who will be the witnesses at your ceremony?"

"I suppose the vicar will have a neighbor he can call upon," Adriana replied with a shrug.

Sophia shook her head adamantly. "It's all wrong. Bess would want to come. And our brothers."

Adriana bit her lip. "It's better if they don't know. That way, Papa cannot take out his anger on them."

Sophia had no quick reply. No comfort to offer her sister. No lie she could tell herself. The future with her father would be even bleaker now.

Freddy and Adriana stood with hands clasped tightly together, hope and apprehension displayed in equal measure upon their features. Sophia did not know what to do.

What would Tobias do?

The answer was easy. He would ignore all the negative voices—hers, society's—and seize the day. After all, Adriana was only going to marry once.

Sophia squared her shoulders.

"What about me?" she asked. "I could go. I know about the wedding already. If Papa does discover this, he will withhold the greatest measure of his wrath for the sake of my health." She thought wryly of the irony. Never before had her weakened condition offered her an advantage. "I should be there," she continued. "*Someone* from our family should be there for you, Deedee. You deserve at least that much!"

"I wish that with all my heart!" Adriana cried. "But the journey would be too strenuous for you. And then walking up the path into the church… It would be too much. I feel enough guilt as it is. Let's not make it worse."

"A footman could carry me. Goodness knows they do it often enough. And my carriage ride with Tobias did me no end of good. I am not tired at all."

"I don't think racing up the stairs helped," Adriana said with a frown. "You've had a shock. You should rest."

"Fine." Sophia crossed her arms. "Bring me a chair. And a cup of tea. I'll rest for twenty minutes and then we'll leave."

"Oh, you are impossible!" Adriana laughed. She wagged her finger at Tobias. "This is your doing. Beware the monster you have created. As a child, she was a force to be reckoned with. I see her old self is rapidly returning under your influence."

Tobias had not said a word during the entire exchange between the sisters. Even now, he asked no questions and offered no judgment. But he did have an opinion, and he voiced it now.

"I will not pretend to understand why you feel it necessary to elope, Miss Grant. And I do not feel this is the time to ask for explanations. But Sophia is quite right, of course. She should be in attendance at your nuptials." He cleared his throat. "If it will give you any measure of relief, I would like to offer myself as her companion. I will escort her home again after the service and make certain she is delivered safely to Katie's care." He cast a loving glance toward Sophia. "I do this, not only for the memories you will make together today, but also so that she may have someone with whom to recall them in the future. Such joy must be shared again and again to experience its full measure. I cannot imagine greater frustration than having a cherished recollection of your wedding day and being unable to reminisce about it with anyone."

Adriana touched Tobias softly on his sleeve. "You are a wise man, Mr. Mannerly, and a generous soul. You have no idea how grateful I am that Sophia will have you to turn to in my absence."

"Does that mean you will permit me to be your guest today?"

"Permit? Freddy and I would be delighted!"

Freddy nodded in agreement, but his face was serious. "I am sorry your family will be hurt by this, Sophia. Believe me, it is not what we wanted."

"You are not to blame," Sophia replied. "And you are part of this family now, whether Papa accepts it or not."

Adriana threw her arms around Sophia. "It is good to see your confidence return," she whispered in her ear. "May it give you the courage to claim what is yours."

Long after the warmth of that embrace had faded, and the travel chest was loaded, and the church bells rang out the newlywed bliss of Mr. and Mrs. Frederick Wynn, Sophia would remember her sister's words, hugging them to herself as if Adriana herself were hidden in each syllable.

She had yet to realize how much she would need them.

CHAPTER TWELVE

SETTLED AT LAST at the front of the small, stone church, Sophia could enjoy her view of the happy couple. The way the room had shrunk to contain just the two of them. How Freddy held her gaze in his, her hand and heart in his.

Adriana was wearing her favorite winter dress, a long-sleeved, powder-pink creation with very little adornment. Mama had always said Adriana's personality was all the ornament she ever needed. This was never truer than today. Her face shone with joy. And peace—a feature that seldom made its appearance. But it was here now, in abundance.

A pale-brown mink stole kept the cold from her shoulders and back. But her heart—oh, her heart was warmed with love well met. It radiated from her like the glow of a brave new dawn.

As lovely as her sister looked, Sophia knew it had little to do with her attire. Regardless of what she wore, Adriana would shine today. In this moment, all sorrows of the past, all fears of the future, were quite forgotten. Freddy would join his life to hers, bandage the wounds not yet healed or yet to be formed. It was a moment of unalloyed hope. And it was contagious.

Sophia tilted her head toward Tobias. He was that man for her. The one who made her forget lingering pain and replaced it with dreams she had long believed impossible. Sometimes she even pictured those dreams coming true. If anyone could bring rebirth to her father's fossilized emotions, it would be Tobias. Look how the scars in her own heart had faded! Perhaps, given enough time, she would be standing in this very church, with her father's blessing, hearing the parish priest say…

"I pronounce that they be man and wife together."

Freddy and Adriana turned to face the handful of witnesses, grinning unabashedly.

Somewhere from the back of the church came a gasp, followed by a muffled laugh.

"Shush, Mary. People will stare." The low voice sounded more bored than dismayed.

"But, Irene, that's Miss Adriana Grant!"

"I believe she is Mrs. Wynn now."

"No, you don't understand." The woman called Mary spoke in a whisper so loud that the small church echoed with her words. "She's the daughter of Mr. Conrad Grant. You know. *Him.* The one who lost his wife and then lost his mind."

Freddy and Adriana froze. The fresh matrimonial bliss drained from their faces.

"Ah," said the woman called Irene, sounding decidedly more enthusiastic, "then we simply *must* go and shake their hands."

A rustling of skirts preceded the soft patter of eager feet up the aisle. As the two women hurried past, one of them glanced down at Sophia and Tobias and—seeming to recognize no one of value—continued on. But her narrow face and regal air would be burned forever into Sophia's memory.

The other woman—far prettier, but lacking the same presence as her imposing friend—did not even acknowledge their presence. She was far too keen to reach the unfortunate newlyweds, her arms extended in ready embrace, her face a mask of celebration.

Tobias sat bolt upright in the pew. He stared as the mysterious woman hugged Adriana and pulled away, only to grab her hands instead in pretended friendship.

"Why, Mrs. Wynn, I did not expect to see you under such

pleasant circumstances." The stranger whirled around as if struck by a sudden thought. "Your father is not here?" Her triumph at finding Sophia and Adriana's father absent was ill-disguised. But her surprise at seeing Tobias was not concealed at all.

"Mr. Mannerly! What are *you* doing here? And who is this with you? Are you friends of the bride or groom?"

Tobias looked as if he wished to shrink inside his coat.

"Are you not going to introduce us, sir?" the woman asked, an almost predatory smile lacing her eyes and mouth.

"So this is Mr. Mannerly?" the tall, haughty friend inquired, her expression no less hungry. "Yes, now I understand. You described him perfectly, Mary." Her lips curled into a condescending smile. "And with whom does Mr. Mannerly keep company now?"

She stepped toward Sophia, her very fashionable dress shaping around bony knees that matched the rest of her equally angular features. She dropped her hand limply at Sophia's face, as if she expected to have it kissed in papal fashion. "Irene Sangford." She announced herself, her voice a languid drawl, as though she could scarcely be bothered to make the effort of speech. "And you are?"

Sophia felt obliged to shake the rather forward woman's hand, though her gentle grip was not returned. It was akin to greeting a fish—all cool and damp, and *sans* an ounce of character.

Tobias stood up, forcing Miss Sangford to take a step backward. "You will know Miss Sophia Grant from her great works of poetry. And we are here to support both bride and groom."

He looked grimly at Sophia. "These ladies are Miss Irene Sangford, whom I have just met, and Miss Mary Dunbar, with whom I am previously acquainted."

"Miss Sophia Grant?" Miss Dunbar swiveled to face her. "I was given to understand you never left the sanctuary of your home. Is your health so greatly improved, then, that attending your sister's wedding does it no harm?"

Miss Sangford snickered. "Isn't it obvious? Mr. Mannerly is clearly the cause for her newly robust constitution."

Tobias hastily interjected. "And which of the wedding party have *you* come to support?"

"Why, my own!" Miss Dunbar cried. "We came to discuss the details of the forthcoming event with Mr. Darrow here." She indicated the clergyman who waited patiently for their appointment to proceed. "We were early. Or your wedding ran late. What does it matter? We bothered no one. Merely sat in the last pew and waited." She barked a quick laugh. "Not in a month of Sundays did we expect the Grants at a wedding. Nor *in* a wedding, for that matter." The hunter's lust returned to her eyes. "And we certainly did not know of your connection to their…*remarkable* family."

"Nor was it necessary for you to know," Tobias replied stiffly. "We no longer frequent the same society, you and I."

Miss Dunbar cocked her head to the side. "Did we ever really, though? After a few appearances at card evenings and dances, you rarely left your uncle's home anymore. Lord Carthige must be *ever* such fascinating company." A smirk escaped and she looked away before Mr. Darrow spied it.

Miss Sangford, by contrast, drew nearer, as if pulled by a magnet.

"Lord Carthige? The earl is your uncle?"

Tobias nodded curtly.

"Oh my, I had no idea we were in such illustrious company."

"You are not," Tobias answered. "I am merely a student of books. I do not stand to inherit the title or the estate."

"No." Miss Sangford appeared thoughtful. "That would go to his son."

"If he ever has one." Miss Dunbar shrugged. "Lord Carthige is something of a recluse, isn't he, Mr. Mannerly? I believe there is a younger brother who will receive all eventually."

"A married brother," added Miss Sangford with a tone of disapproval.

"Well, yes," her friend agreed. "And just as well. Else what would happen to the family line?"

"The situation can yet be salvaged," declared Miss Sangford. "While Lord Carthige lives, an heir can be procured."

The thought of Miss Sangford anywhere near Lord Carthige, with her claws extended and ready to sink in, roused the mother tigress in Sophia.

"He is happy as he is," she informed the presumptuous woman. After all, hadn't Tobias told her as much already in their earliest correspondence? His uncle was apparently the most content fellow Tobias had ever had the pleasure to know.

Miss Sangford raised a bemused eyebrow. "Is he, indeed? It is my experience that men do not know what they want. It is up to the fairer sex to enlighten them."

"I need no one to tell me my own mind," Tobias snapped. "And neither does my uncle."

"My dear Mr. Mannerly, your own mind has led you into an intrigue with a daughter of Mr. Conrad Grant." She turned to indicate the now-simmering Adriana but stopped when Tobias's eyes flicked to Sophia instead.

"I see!" she gloated. "There are *two* secrets revealed today! And here I thought this would be a dull meeting to discuss my friend's nuptials."

Behind her, Mr. Darrow cleared his throat meaningfully. "Speaking of which, Miss Dunbar, should we proceed to the rectory? I can take notes for the arrangements in my study. And the chairs are more comfortable than our pews."

"You go ahead, Mary dear," Miss Sangford purred. "I shall amuse myself here instead."

Mr. Darrow frowned. "May I remind you, Miss Sangford, that this is a house of God? It is not a venue for superficial entertainment."

"Why, Mr. Darrow, I merely wish to further my acquaintance with these darling souls of your flock. You would not begrudge me that, would you?"

"My wife can offer you a hot cup of tea and a warm parlor instead," he tried again.

"I am in need of neither," she said.

"I wish you would come with me, Irene," Miss Dunbar complained. "You have such a good mind for details. That is why I asked you in the first place."

"Oh, I shall be along presently," her friend replied without even looking at her. "There are just a few arrangements to be made here first."

Miss Dunbar paused, her eyes flitting from Miss Sangford to Tobias. "Don't waste your time on a lost cause, dear."

"Oh, I think I have it all in hand, thank you." Miss Sangford formed a terrifyingly friendly smile that lurked like a stranger upon her face.

"Very well. But do be quick. I quite rely on your sharp mind to steer me through all that must be done."

Miss Sangford nodded, sustaining her smile with remarkable skill until Mr. Darrow escorted Miss Dunbar through the doors of the church. Then, it folded in upon itself. And the prowling hunger was back.

"How dare you!" Adriana flew at her, seething with rage. "How dare you insert yourself into our company and spoil our day! You are not welcome here!"

"What?" The smile returned, but it was not friendly. "You wish to banish me from this sanctuary? That is rather presumptuous, don't you think?"

"No more presumptuous than your insinuations about our family and that of Lord Carthige." Adriana's fists were balled. She had them primed at her side. One wrong word from Miss Sangford and she would very likely need to be held back. Freddy put a protective hand on his wife's arm, though Sophia knew it was Miss Sangford who was truly in danger.

Tobias stepped between them. "I think it best if you go, Miss Sangford. There is nothing for you here."

"Oh, I disagree," replied the harpy. And she sat down.

The tension in the room thickened.

She patted the pew. "Please, do join me. We have much to discuss."

"We will do nothing of the sort." Freddy growled. "Come, Adriana, we must get your sister home before…"

"Before your father knows she is missing?" Miss Sangford inquired innocently.

"It is none of your business," Adriana hissed. "Return to your friend and your menial amusements. Leave us alone."

"You do not give me enough credit, Mrs. Wynn. Come. Sit down. Let me explain my little scheme to you."

Sophia's chest tightened. Warning signals chased up her spine, and dread seeped into every limb. This woman was dangerous. Of that, she had no doubt. She could see the fear in Adriana's eyes, despite her fury. And if Adriana was afraid, it was very bad indeed.

When no one moved, Miss Sangford sighed. "Very well, stay as you are. It makes no difference to me." She picked at an imaginary speck on her skirt, flicked it away, then folded her hands upon her lap to signify readiness.

"You have married without Mr. Grant's blessing," she said matter-of-factly. "Nay, I would go so far as to say, without his knowledge. Your sister is co-conspirator. And Mr. Mannerly is unknown to him entirely. How am I doing so far?"

Sophia squirmed with the accuracy of these deductions. Her companions stood rooted to the spot, waiting for their accuser to reveal her intent.

"What of it?" Adriana managed to say, though her voice was unable to match the nonchalance of her words.

"Certainly, you expect your father to discover the elopement. No doubt you have a brave spirit, Mrs. Wynn. I admire that. But he would be doubly betrayed if he knew your sister had attended the wedding behind his back. And one can only guess at the heights of wrath he would reach if Mr. Mannerly's role were discovered."

"*Blackmail?* You want to blackmail us?" Tobias uttered a gruff laugh. "Do your worst. I am not afraid of Mr. Grant."

"No?" Irene Sangford rounded on Sophia like a cobra, pinning her down with the threat of the poison she had in her bite. "I think Miss Grant does not share your sentiment. Do you, Miss Grant? Perhaps, instead, you writhe with fear at the very thought of being thus exposed. I would wager you would do anything, *anything*, to keep this from happening." Her head whipped around so suddenly that Tobias jumped a little in spite of himself. "And you would do anything for your beloved if she asked you, would you not, hmmm?"

Tobias straightened his waistcoat. "What do you want, exactly?"

Miss Sangford clapped her hands and brought them to her chin. "I'm so glad you asked. It is only a very small thing." Her eyes flashed with avarice. "I would like an introduction to the earl."

"What on Earth for?" Tobias exclaimed.

"Oh, you have wholly overestimated yourself, Miss Sangford." Adriana sneered. "The earl will want nothing to do with the likes of you."

Adriana's words had no effect on her opponent's confidence. "We shall see," she answered with infuriating calm. "Lord Carthige is not a man of the world. He is unpracticed in the social arts. I, on the other hand, know the rules of the game and have played it many times."

"And yet you remain unwed," Adriana bit back.

For a moment, something flickered behind Miss Irene Sangford's eyes. It was quickly shuttered again. What was it? Doubt? Humiliation? Sophia did not know. The moment was gone and the weakness hidden.

"It is to my advantage to refuse all offers that are beneath me," Miss Sangford said. "But an earl will do nicely."

"What do you expect will happen?" Adriana continued. "Do you honestly believe Lord Carthige will give up decades of self-imposed seclusion to be bound to such a pasty, bracket-faced scrag? You must be joking!"

Miss Sangford leaped from her seat, thrusting a bony finger under Adriana's nose. "You know nothing! Men are fools!" In a heartbeat, the inflamed woman subsided into something resembling charm. "Oh, my dear Lord Carthige…" She simpered. "I had not realized there was someone who shared my preoccupation…nay, my *obsession* with books. Why, yes, I would love to see your library. No, I am in no rush. I am content in your company, surrounded by such great volumes." She straightened up, resuming her usual demeanor. "Do you see?" She opened her palm. "I hold out the seed, and the little bird is in my hand."

Tobias clenched his jaw. "He is neither infirm of mind nor body. You will be transparent as glass. And if he should grant you any leniency, I would be sure to correct his thinking."

"Oh, but you won't. If you speak, I speak." She threw a glance at Sophia. "Ask her if she has the strength for the truth. Go ahead. I can wait."

Tobias turned his distraught face to Sophia, who shriveled under his gaze. "Sophia? Would it matter so much?"

She turned her head away. She could not look him in the eye.

Adriana touched his shoulder. "Please, she is not yet strong enough. Maybe, in time. But not today. It will break what little spirit she has regained."

Tobias scowled. "So, I must trust my uncle not to fall prey to this…this…monstrous thing?"

Sophia burst into tears, burying her face in her hands. "I am so sorry, Tobias." She had no words for him. None of her studies, none of the numerous languages she had mastered, had given her the right speech for a situation like this. There wasn't a single line of poetry that could counter the depths of her guilt or the depravity of her enemy.

She felt her beloved's eyes upon her, waiting for her support. Waiting in vain. Then his gaze lifted, and she heard him say, "Very well. An introduction shall be made. For the good it will do you."

"Capital! You have one month to arrange it. Or Mr. Grant receives a letter from a concerned member of the public, detailing your various subterfuges. There are likely more I have not yet uncovered. You will decide how motivated I am to do so."

There was a heavy silence as the threat sank in.

It was disturbed by Frederick Wynn clearing his throat uncomfortably.

"I don't mean to make this damnable affair any worse, but how, exactly, are we to arrange this? What is the excuse Mr. Mannerly should rely on to invite Miss Sangford to Newcliffe Hall? We all know Lord Carthige is unlikely to be drawn from his home. Nor would he expect his nephew to be friends with Miss Sangford. Especially since his lordship is aware of his affections for Miss Grant."

"Well, there you have your solution," said Miss Sangford. "Arrange the introduction through Miss Grant. She must surely have lady friends to tea. Invite the earl along. He is your neighbor, after all." She rolled her eyes. "Really, must I do all the thinking for you?"

"You don't understand," Tobias argued. "Mr. Grant is not accustomed to..."

Miss Sangford held up her hand. "I am becoming rather bored of your lack of imagination, sir. And my friend is waiting for me. You have one month. You may be sure I shall not forget our arrangement. Meanwhile, I bid you adieu." And she sailed from the room, leaving devastation in her wake.

CHAPTER THIRTEEN

TOBIAS AND SOPHIA parted from the newlyweds at the posting inn, where Adriana sat glumly on her travel trunk while Freddy made arrangements to hire a coach to take them to their new, shared home. The excitement that had underpinned the day was now undone, all the joy siphoned from it by that quenchless vampire, Miss Irene Sangford.

The sisters hugged each other, an embrace of support, sorrow, and final farewell. Their tearful parting may have lingered indefinitely, but necessity abbreviated its course. Time was running out. Mr. Grant would soon be home.

Tobias still could not fathom what sort of man necessitated one daughter to elope and the other to witness it in fearful secrecy. As far as he could tell, Freddy Wynn was a man of good character, with the promise of a steady income and a family who supported his choices. It seemed odd that Mr. Grant could not accept him as a match for Adriana. Sophia certainly did. Mr. Grant must have been some sort of ogre if his daughters could not share the truth of their affections with him. Tobias would have to wrangle an explanation from Sophia, but this was neither the time nor place.

Amid assurances of daily letters, Sophia was bundled into the waiting carriage, exhausted in body and mind. Tobias accompanied her, as promised, though he sensed his presence no longer held the comfort it might have done when he had given the promise originally.

It was a far cry from their earlier ride of the morning. As the wheels kicked into motion, Sophia sank into the darkest corner of the compartment. She had not uttered a word to him since they'd left the church. Though spring continued to bloom gently outside, and birds made their presence known through song, the interior of the carriage was gloomy and silent.

"Sophia," Tobias said softly. Then again, "Sophia," in a firmer tone.

She would not look at him.

"You will have to talk to me sooner or later."

The shadowed figure remained mute.

"Can we not speak of your father?"

There was no answer.

"This cannot continue. Why do you fear him so?"

"I do not fear him."

The reply did not invite discussion. Tobias pushed on, carefully.

"Why, then, must we comply with Miss Sangford's wicked scheme? We have a whole month in which to respond to her demands. In that time, we could speak to your father and explain…"

Sophia shook her head, a whimper escaping from her throat.

"No? You say *no*, and yet you will not explain yourself. What am I to make of that, Sophia?"

"I am sorry."

Tobias huffed a sigh of frustration.

"Look, we are in this together, no matter what. But you have to help me, my darling. Is there nothing that can make it easier to approach your father? If I proved myself in some way? If we had more time? Perhaps, if Miss Sangford could be persuaded to give us another month…"

"It would make no difference," Sophia said, her voice so quiet, it was scarcely audible. "It is quite impossible to reason with him."

Tobias threw his hands in the air and sat back. "I confess, I am at a loss. You will neither clarify the problem nor assist in the solution. What am I to make of this, Sophia?"

She released a shaky breath. "I understand. You have done your best. No one can fault you. You deserve better."

His caution dissolved in an instant. "Oh, no, you don't!" Tobias leaned forward once more, grasping Sophia's hand. "You will not withdraw from me again!"

"Release me, Tobias." She squirmed, trying to free her hand.

"I will not!" He took both her hands instead and pulled them toward him, compelling Sophia to rouse from her refuge.

Her chin lifted and her eyes flew open. "Leave me, Tobias. I am no good for you."

"I'll be the judge of that."

"You could have any woman of your choosing. They would be lucky to…"

"I don't want anybody else. You are far rarer a being than you give yourself credit for. There are too many Miss Dunbars in the world, and not enough Sophia Grants."

Sophia lowered her eyes again. "Perhaps. But the Miss Dunbars of the world still have their weddings."

"Much good it will do her husband." Tobias scoffed. "Though he is probably just like her. Pompous and vain. Good luck to them, I say. I would far rather fight for you." A happy image bubbled to the surface. "I can see it clearly," he told her. "Your lovely neck bent over a new poem while my uncle and I savor the contents of his library. The three of us sharing a meal and discussing our favorite Greek philosophers. Private carriage rides whenever we please." His voice grew husky. "Perhaps, if you feel strong enough, we might even have a babe of our own."

But Sophia's eyes did not grow dreamy at these thoughts.

"You said you would be patient." Her voice was thick with reprimand.

Tobias sighed and released her hands.

"So I did." He sat and pondered the sad picture that was his beloved. Blast that Sangford woman! Weeks of progress gone in a flash. Sophia had crawled right back into her cocoon. And he was no nearer to understanding why. Perhaps it was time to ask his uncle what he knew.

Dear Uncle Edmund. His heart sank. There was another pretty mess—betraying a man who was like a father to him. Even though his uncle was quite safe from that devil-woman's wiles—and Tobias needed to believe that—it felt wrong to keep secrets from him. Subterfuge did not come naturally to Tobias. It was bad enough that his relationship with Sophia was necessarily covert. But even this secret had been shared with Uncle Edmund. Tobias had needed a sensible confidant. And his uncle was certainly sensible. There was no reason to suspect that Miss Sangford stood a chance against his cool logic.

Tobias recalled her little show of practiced charm. Her performance had come so easily, unbound by scruples, strengthened by a cold determination to obtain her selfish desires. What if... He swallowed hard. What if Miss Sangford found a chink in his uncle's armor? Tobias shuddered. The idea was too terrible. He could not bear it. He was grateful when Sophia's small voice sounded from the corner in which she had ensconced herself.

"I don't understand," she said with simple honesty. "Why do you persist, even now, when it all seems hopeless? I give you no encouragement, and yet you will not give up."

Tobias hesitated. It was true. Sophia had discouraged him at every turn. And yet, he had caught her secret glances, the ones that shone with affection, her eyes filled with trust and, yes, desire. He had begun to peel back the layers of resistance she had shrouded herself in. Beneath it all, he knew, her heart pulsed a slow and steady tattoo for him. But ripples of fear and distrust disguised it. He needed to help her understand how deep the current of his own feelings ran.

Slowly, he stood and stepped across the narrow space between them to sit beside her.

"Why do you love to write poetry?" he asked.

"Oh," she said, her mouth round with surprise. And then, with a rush of confidence, she added, "Because it gives me purpose. It makes me happy. I feel most myself when I am wrestling with just the right words. It adds meaning to a world that is otherwise very stark and lonely at times." Her cheeks colored with a surge of feeling.

Tobias closed his eyes and breathed in as though he had just perceived the sweetest perfume. Then he opened them again and smiled warmly. "Yes, dearest Sophia. That is it exactly. *You* are my poetry."

Sophia seemed to consider this. It was encouragement enough that she had not rejected his statement out of hand.

"I...I cannot imagine my life without poetry," she answered at last. "It is not a situation I could flourish in."

"Just so." He beamed.

"I have sacrificed my time and energy to it willingly."

"They have been well invested."

"But I have never sacrificed another for this privilege," she pointed out. "And you should not have to do so for me. Your uncle is a good man. And your future with him is secure. I cannot offer you the same guarantee with me."

"And yet," Tobias persisted, "if your art were to be wrenched from you..." His hands mimicked the action. "If it were to be lost, unless you offered up another part of yourself? Would the decision really be that difficult? Surely, the smaller sacrifice is more bearable than the greater?"

"I suppose that would depend."

"Perhaps, a month of no letters from Adriana?"

"That would be hard."

"But not unbearable? Not like losing that which is entwined in your heart?"

"No."

"Then you understand me."

Sophia was silent awhile. Tobias did not press her. He could not make his feelings any clearer. It was up to her to accept them.

"I am your poetry," she repeated to herself. She looked up at Tobias. "These are weighty words."

"I fully understand what I mean by them. Do you?"

"Will your uncle not suffer for your choice?"

Tobias swallowed. "I do not believe him to be a desperate man. He will not be swayed by false charms. If any pain is caused, it will be when he discovers my deception."

"Must he?"

Tobias nodded. "When Miss Sangford's scheme has failed, and she returns beneath the slimy rock from which she has slithered, I will confess all to him." He stared out through the carriage window, across fields that cared not for his future and could offer him no solace. "He may punish me as he sees fit." His gaze returned to Sophia, where he might find comfort.

She spoke at once with concern. "This is a great risk, Tobias. What if you lose your place with your uncle at Newcliffe Hall? It has been home and sustenance to you."

"I could take up a position as tutor. Or work as a clerk. I might not earn very much, but I have the necessary qualifications."

"You would hate that!"

"I have faith it will not come to that. But I owe it to my uncle to reveal the truth when it is safe to do so."

"If you revealed it now, it would spare you both suffering."

"I will not spare myself only to have you suffer instead. Miss Sangford must leave your family be."

Sophia chewed on her lip.

Tobias held his breath.

"Very well," she agreed.

Tobias exhaled with relief.

"On one condition."

He offered her a wary glance. "What is it?"

"If there is any indication that his lordship is falling into Miss Sangford's trap, we must rescue him from it, no matter the cost."

Tobias sucked in a rush of air. "That would mean…"

"Yes, I know what it means. But I don't think *you* do. When she reveals the truth, the result will not merely be an uncomfortable confrontation with my father."

"No?"

"No." Sophia's fingers clasped and unclasped each other with nervous energy. "There would be no more…poetry."

"Oh. But we could still…"

"It would be quite impossible."

"I see." Now it was Tobias who was solemn and silent.

"Do you accept my condition?"

"It is a heavy price."

"Yes, my love. It is."

Sophia looked up into his eyes. Her own were wide and hopeful, but she bit her lip tentatively.

"I will not have your uncle pay the price for a secret that was never his to bargain for," Sophia insisted, though her chin trembled a little as she said so. "This is the pact I am willing to make. Shake my hand and seal it like a gentleman."

Tobias reached out and took her precious hand in his. "You have my word."

Sophia released a shuddering breath. At once, Tobias pressed her to him, her ear upon his pounding heart. Her bonnet pushed back and he gently undid its ribbon, freeing the beautiful frame of her face from its stiff enclosure. He stroked her curls, soothing himself in equal measure with each caress.

"We will weather this storm," he assured her, in the hopes of also reassuring himself.

They sat in this manner, drawing courage from each other. The movement of the carriage both jostled and lulled the lovers within. Sophia's breathing became more even, and Tobias allowed himself a few treasured moments of pleasure, his beloved within his embrace, the world outside a distant place that touched them not.

It was simple and wonderful, and it ended rather abruptly

when Sophia pushed herself upright, crying, "I have it!"

"What is it?" Tobias asked, trying to quiet his racing pulse at the suddenness of her action.

"The invitation! You haven't forgotten, surely? There must be a means of bringing Miss Sangford and Lord Carthige under the same roof."

To be perfectly honest—Tobias admitted to himself only—the issue of the invitation had quite escaped him while Sophia rested in his arms. The scent of his beloved still lingered in his mind, as did the memory of her hair teasing his chin. His happy thoughts tried to shuffle aside to accommodate the urgency of this new conversation, but did so rather grudgingly.

"You have an idea?" He marveled that she had found a solution, especially since one of his own was entirely absent.

"I do. Though really it was you who gave it to me.'

"I did?" Tobias was genuinely puzzled.

But Sophia was already rushing ahead in the conversation.

"Of course, I alone cannot carry out this plan," she said, her manner businesslike and serious. "However, you have access to a resource that is perfectly suited."

"Oh, good," Tobias enthused rather weakly.

"It is the one excuse for which Father will tolerate company, especially if it is to include me."

Tobias perked up at once. "What is it? Tell me. What has your brilliant mind conjured up?"

Sophia clasped her hands together and brought them to her lips, which broadened into a smile.

"Poetry, Tobias," she declared. Poetry."

CHAPTER FOURTEEN

A FEW DAYS later, Lord Carthige found his nephew pacing in the entrance hall.

"He will be along in his own time, Tobias. I do not see what you hope to achieve by wearing out your shoes on the marble."

"He did say eight o'clock, did he not?" Tobias asked, checking the wall clock for the fifth time.

"It is barely ten minutes past the hour. Do settle down. A man of his position is entitled to be fashionably late."

"I rather got the impression he preferred punctuality," Tobias countered.

Edmund Stopford regarded his nephew with some suspicion. "And I was under the impression you did not care for him a great deal. Yet here you are, like a puppy, waiting to meet your master at the door."

Tobias stopped his tireless traverse of the foyer. "Perhaps I was a little hasty in my judgement," he admitted. "Lord Howell is a gentleman of culture. And intellect. He has revealed as much in his appreciation for Sophia's talents."

"Dear boy…" Uncle Edmund shook his head. "You really do lack the subtleties of fine society. I must insist you not overwhelm our guest with your fondness for Miss Grant. After all, he is here to further the matters of his own heart."

"And I have just the thing to rally the ladies to his cause."

His uncle raised an eyebrow. "Indeed? This is most unexpected. I did not realize you had taken it upon yourself to help Lord Howell. It is very generous, Tobias. You are a good fellow."

A good fellow. Tobias's skin itched with guilt. His uncle was so trusting. And why should he not be? Nothing but respect and true companionship had ever passed between them. Now plots were made under the earl's own roof. And he, Tobias, was a willing participant.

"Er…thank you, Uncle," he replied. "Though to be honest"— *How he wished he could speak the truth to its fullest!*—"my motives are selfish and intended more to help Miss Grant."

This *was* the truth, was it not? But Tobias knew his words had been carefully chosen to mislead. It shamed him deeply.

"I suppose," his uncle said after a moment's reflection, "you cannot help yourself. You will always put your heart before your head. It is often so in one's youth."

Although Tobias was weighted with remorse for his pending actions, his ego was pricked by his uncle's words. "I'd like to think my heart will always be my true north," he said, trying not to sound too defensive. "If that changed with age, my character would have to change also. Those of us who do not wish to live alone will always be led by our hearts."

"I do not live alone," Uncle Edmund pointed out. "I have chosen your company. And I have come to love you like a son. Yet I still have a clear mind, first and foremost."

"Yes, Uncle, that is exactly my point. You have always been thus."

"Have I?"

Somewhat taken aback, Tobias stared at his uncle, trying to make sense of his meaning. "That was my understanding," he added. "That you chose this quiet life. That is why you have no heir, and your brother will inherit after you."

A strange sadness descended upon his uncle's features, a softening of his usually very controlled expression. "I suppose you are right," he said with a deep weariness. "In a way, I did choose this. Yes, I can see why you would think that."

A sliver of pure ice slid down Tobias's spine, making the hair on his arms stand up in alarm. Had he gotten it wrong somehow? Did his uncle long for love? Had he merely given up, subsiding into this secluded lifestyle? And oh—terrible, nightmarish thought!—might Miss Sangford worm her way into that lonely space his uncle had almost forgotten existed?

The knock at the door made Tobias jump.

"Come, come, Nephew." His uncle smiled, though it was once again the smile he reserved for the purpose of expressing kindness. A smile originating in thought rather than sentiment. An act of self-control, to choose which emotion to release at the desired time. It left Tobias feeling unsettled. What unreached tides of feeling lay in the reservoir of his uncle's heart? What if Miss Sangford found the sluice and released the floodwaters?

Lord Howell entered and the footman closed the heavy oak door behind him. While the butler greeted him and the footman took the viscount's coat and hat, Tobias tried to pull himself together. The evening had just begun and there was much at stake. But the uneasiness would not recede.

Fortunately, Uncle Edmund was not hamstrung thus and, waving the servants away, walked calmly with his guest to the drawing room. Tobias trailed behind, fretting and nervous, and anxious to appear as neither.

They seated themselves in front of the blazing fire. Lord Howell dwarfed the chair he had chosen, though to be fair, none of the furniture in the drawing room was designed to accommodate a man of his physique. This was not the case for Uncle Edmund, whose favorite chair was all but molded to his shape after years of use. Comfortably ensconced, he reached for his glasses and a stack of letters on the side table.

"I have had a considerable response," he began. "My sister and her friends have been most industrious in their efforts to ascertain the existence and whereabouts of appropriate candidates. All with great discretion, of course."

"That is good news, I suppose," Lord Howell answered without much enthusiasm.

Uncle Edmund removed his glasses. "My dear Howell, we proceed at your pleasure. If you have changed your mind..."

"No, no, needs must." Lord Howell spread his fingers over his knee and gave a short, sharp huff of frustration. "It is just such a damnable nuisance to be shopping for a bride when there are more urgent matters that demand my attention daily."

"No doubt, when Lady Howell takes her place at your side, you will find these matters less irksome."

"If you say so, Carthige." The viscount shrugged. "Though it is hard to imagine drawing comfort from a stranger."

"She will not be a stranger by the time you wed. A proper courtship will resolve this in a matter of months."

"And if I have chosen unwisely? It's not exactly like a meat pie that one can discard if the filling is not found to one's taste."

"Er, no." Uncle Edmund, rather flustered at such an image, was momentarily put off his stride.

The fire crackled and spat. The viscount, by contrast, lacked any vigor. To Tobias, it was clear the man was seeking a partnership he neither craved nor relished.

"Ideally," Tobias said, entering the conversation gingerly, "one would want the opportunity to meet these ladies before they are aware that they are... How did my uncle put it? Ah, yes. *Candidates.*"

"Certainly," Uncle Edmund agreed. "It would put your mind at ease to determine who among them has, er... suitable filling." He cleared his throat quite noisily to express his evident discomfort with his friend's earlier expression. "What did you have in mind, Tobias? A ball?"

Tobias shook his head. The viscount—who had visibly tensed at the suggestion—sagged with relief. "Dancing is not to everyone's taste. And the opportunity for meaningful conversation is limited, in my opinion. No, what we need is something to draw the interest of more refined ladies. Women who would prefer something intellectual. You are more likely to find a suitable match where your interests are shared."

"Go on." Lord Howell nodded, his interest piqued at last.

"Of course, if you hosted the event, the invitation to these ladies would come from you. That is not subtle."

The now-characteristic blush appeared on the viscount's cheeks. "Indeed, I would prefer to observe without obvious motive."

"So, what we need is an intellectual event where your attendance would be considered natural and which would be attractive to women of sound education and promising character. We will have their aunts and cousins reach out to them with an open invitation. I doubt any will refuse once they know you will be there."

The viscount tapped his finger to his lips, his gaze focused on a space several feet beyond his chair. "Hmm, I can see you have given this much thought, Mr. Mannerly. I doubt Carthige and I would have been as innovative."

"I am happy to help, my lord. The search for love is a worthwhile endeavor."

Lord Howell looked across at his friend, the earl. "I had not expected love to play a role at all. A degree of compatibility would be sufficient. Someone I did not detest before the year was out."

"Forgive me, sir," Tobias objected, "but that is a poor outcome indeed. If the intention is to have an heir…well…surely, it is not enough simply to tolerate your bride? If you'll pardon my bluntness for saying so."

The viscount tipped his head in Tobias's direction but addressed the earl. "Passionate fellow, isn't he? Probably wouldn't do to tell him that my entire ancestral line was made in this fashion."

Tobias was far from discouraged. Despite his lordship's wry humor on the subject, everything was proceeding swimmingly. One or two more details, and the deal was done. They might even find the viscount the perfect wife in the process. He was almost giddy with the thrill of it.

"I feel optimistic that your hopes will fare better than your expectations," he told Lord Howell. "We shall certainly give it our best effort. Needless to say, my uncle and I will attend to offer you courage and support."

He had slipped it in quickly, hoping to sound casual, counting on Lord Howell to accept their loyal presence before his uncle could protest.

There was a brief, pointed look from Lord Carthige. "I would thank my nephew to let me speak for myself."

Tobias froze. His head filled with a roar of blood.

"However, he is right."

The pounding in his ears subsided.

"There is no question. We will accompany you, of course. Especially if the occasion is to be stimulating to the mind." He glanced at Tobias. "What, exactly, were your thoughts on this?"

Tobias steeled himself. His uncle was going to have definite opinions about this.

"I had in mind a poetry reading by Miss Sophia Grant."

Lord Carthige clenched with obvious disapproval. "Really, Tobias, I hardly think his lordship…"

"No, hear me out, Uncle. I…"

"We are all aware of your enthusiasm for Miss Grant and her artistic skills, but to use my friend's predicament to further her career…"

"That was not my intention at all!"

At Tobias's raised voice, Lord Carthige grew stern. "I am not accustomed to being shouted at in my own home. And in front of a guest, no less. You forget yourself, Nephew."

Tobias fought to control himself. He should apologize. Pace himself. Speak calmly. It was just so infernally frustrating! He loathed the meandering route of polite speech. He wanted to say what needed to be said, work out the practicalities. Not bob and weave through social niceties.

Lord Carthige was still waiting.

Tobias took a bolstering breath.

"I am sorry, sir. I only wanted to assure you that I would never abuse your kindness or hospitality for the sake of Miss Grant."

As he said these words, an immediate heaviness of conscience descended upon him. He half-expected a cockerel to crow at his betrayal.

"I accept you at your word," his uncle replied.

Instead of bringing peace to Tobias, the conciliatory speech was bitter to his ears. He did not deserve it. He burned with shame. But there was to be no reprieve. For he must forge ahead with his plan. He was almost there. And, if it worked, Miss Sangford and the division she wrought would be a thing of the past.

"Actually, Carthige," said Lord Howell, chiming in, "a poetry reading is just the ticket. And if Miss Grant is willing, that is an added blessing. Her caliber of writing will only attract the most discerning audience. I don't know about you, but I hardly have the time to be corresponding with poets and such to see who might be available. This is awfully convenient."

"Yes," Tobias added with happy relief, "we could have the letters sent out tomorrow. Shall we set the date for two weeks hence?" He crossed his fingers inside his coat.

"Two weeks!" His uncle spluttered. "We don't even know if Mr. Grant will allow visitors in his home!"

"Miss Grant has the matter in hand." Tobias spoke boldly, but the truth was that he hadn't the foggiest idea how she would manage it. All he knew was that they had a finite amount of time and everything had to fall into place *just so.*

Lord Carthige muttered his doubts a while longer, while Tobias sought ways to appease them. In the end it was the viscount who set the date. "I don't have any desire to drag this out. The sooner I get it done, the better. Let them come. I shall do my duty."

It was hardly a romantic pledge, but Tobias was grateful, nonetheless. Just because Lord Howell didn't see the promise the occasion held did not mean Tobias shared his pessimism. After all, if Mr. Grant would allow a multitude of strangers into his home, a single suitor a few weeks hence might not, in comparison, seem as arduous a presence. Regardless, they would finally meet. Tobias would be able to get the measure of the man.

All in all, the evening ended well. And, while the two lords pored over the letters, selecting the families who would receive invitations, Tobias sat back and daydreamed about Sophia. Her eyes that drew him in. Her skin like alabaster. And the way the fates were working to bring them to the altar at last.

CHAPTER FIFTEEN

THE DAYS HAD passed rather differently for Sophia. To begin with, her father had returned on Monday to find Adriana gone.

At first he suspected nothing. Adriana was often out. She would take long walks, visit a neighbor for tea, meet with Freddy. Short of locking her in her room, Mr. Grant had given up control of Adriana on Mondays.

But she had always been home before dark.

Being late April, the sun was slower in setting. This far north, the light lingered until after eight in the evening, and Adriana was inclined to use every last second of it.

By half past the hour, the sky had fully darkened, and so had the mood in the home of the Grants. The siblings were questioned. Though no one but Sophia knew the truth, they all grasped at once what had happened. Not a word of it was suggested to their father. He would have to reach that conclusion on his own.

The servants were called in and interrogated. The coachman admitted driving her to church with her luggage but had been led to believe it was a friend's wedding, and that the middle Miss Grant was visiting with the newlyweds for some weeks after.

Her lady's maid was missing. Traveling with her mistress, the coachman explained, to attend to her, as always. Had he misunderstood? His eyes sought Sophia's. A brisk shake of her head, and his loyalty was confirmed. No, there had been no one else.

Sophia watched her father process the information. He understood. He had been betrayed. Abandoned. Such would be his reaction. He would not bewail having missed the ceremony. He would not own the guilt for the extreme measures his daughter had been compelled to take. He would not regret the power he now gave Miss Sangford over two households, even should he be made aware of it.

Sophia saw his anger simmer up from its shallow well. But deeper, much deeper, lay the ink-black despair. He had lost a daughter. That which he feared most had come true. Another part of his heart had been shorn off. Now he would cling tighter than ever to what was left. And drive his precious children even further from him.

The servants were dismissed from his presence. They would not be held accountable. Adriana had protected them with lies. And now Sophia must do the same. She must conspire and manipulate because her father could not be reasoned with. It was the lesser of two evils in Sophia's mind. She blamed Miss Sangford for this difficult choice. She blamed her father. And she blamed herself for not having the strength to stand up to them.

It took her several days to build up the courage to approach her father at all. For better or worse, he did not speak of Adriana. It was as if she had never existed. For the moment, it was simpler this way. Life proceeded with chilling normality. Sophia knew this would take its toll on the family. But for now, it was easier to speak with her father when he was calm, or at least offered the semblance of calm.

Tobias had written the day before. A letter from the Viscount Howell was included. He had done his part. Was she ready to do hers?

Well, of course she wasn't! How could he understand? The truth was, she had never helped him to. It was just so hard to speak of. Painful. Humiliating.

Yet, ready or not, this was the path before her—to convince her father to host a poetry reading on her behalf. It was not going to be easy. But it would be a good degree easier than telling him about Tobias.

In the midst of her nervous symptoms—a churning stomach, and a chest that grew tighter as the moment of action neared—Sophia was amazed to find a flutter of excitement. Certainly, guests in the house were unusual, but Sophia did not have a strong appetite for visitors to begin with. No, the buzz of anticipation was for the eager crowd, headed by the viscount himself, who would be drawn to their home just to hear her read her own words.

It was everything she had ever wanted—to be recognized, validated. And yet, she realized, this alone was not enough. Her world had expanded in the past months. She wanted more. She wanted Tobias. She wanted to share her words with him. To touch *his* mind more than any other. To touch his heart. To touch.

A memory drifted up of his hands upon her waist, his lips seeking hers, their warm breath mingling, their heartbeats merging as if they were one being. That was what she wanted. A life shared, in every way.

Perhaps they might even be blessed with children. Sophia did not know if her body was capable, but she wanted very much to bring more of Tobias into the world, more of his selflessness and courage. She had known so much fear and for so long. If she could lay it down, she would never take it up again. She would run headlong into the future, her arms open wide to receive all the joys that a life with Tobias could bring. *If* she could lay down the fear.

But first, this moment in which she felt very alone. It was only the knowledge that Tobias had already struggled up the same hill with his uncle which she must now climb with her father that gave her the confidence to proceed.

Here he came. To kiss her cheek. To bid her good morning. To inquire after her health. To test that the leash with which he bound her was intact.

Well, today she would test it.

"Good morning, Papa," Sophia began, tilting her head to offer the expected cheek. Everything must be familiar, comfortable. Only that which she asked must challenge him. She must lull him, gently, gently, into a state of complaisance.

Her father strode across the carpeted floor. He was dressed for riding, his long hair tied back in a queue that was no longer fashionable. Then again, so much of her father was stuck in the past.

The kiss was given and received. He stepped back to take in the whole picture that was his eldest daughter. "How is my Sophia today? Did you sleep well?"

"I am as much myself as always," she answered. Cryptic as her reply might seem, her father would understand. After all, how could she say she was well when she was confined to this room, this chair? She was well enough. It would suffice.

"Have you had your breakfast yet?"

"Not yet, Papa."

"I could join you after I have taken my exercise, if you are willing. I will be gone but an hour."

Sophia wanted to say she was hungry now, that she was about to send Katie for her breakfast tray. But she did not. He must suffer no disappointment. Not now. She had much to ask of him. They must begin from a place of agreement.

"I will gladly wait for you. Perhaps we may dine at the table. You will have built up an appetite. And a tray can be so clumsy."

"A fine idea!" He turned to Katie. "See that the table is set. And ask Cook to bring out the blackberry preserves." He smiled at Sophia. He knew it was her favorite.

"Thank you, Papa. You are very thoughtful," she said, and she meant it.

"Anything to make you happy," he answered.

Anything? Sophia bit back the bitter reply. It was easy enough to offer a treat while refusing her the freedom to marry. Like a good dog. *Stay. Good girl! Have some blackberry reserves.*

Her father left the room. And Sophia waited for his return, in thoughtful captivity.

⇥⟫⟩⟨⟨⇤

AN HOUR LATER, they were seated together at the small table in the drawing room. Papa was in a very good mood, even humming a little as he spread butter on his hot crumpet.

Sophia had set aside her grievances for now. That was a battle for another day, if she ever found the courage. Today's skirmish was merely in aid of her poetry. At least, that would be the story she told.

"Papa," she began.

"Hmm?" Her father's voice slipped naturally from a hum to a question.

"I have received a very encouraging letter. Can you guess who sent it?"

Her father paused in the midst of the bite he was about to take. "Is it a publisher?"

"No, not a publisher. Someone more powerful than that."

"Who is more powerful to the artist than their publisher?" her father wanted to know.

"An influential reader," she replied.

"I am intrigued. Is it one of your comrades in poetry? Byron, perhaps? Wordsworth?"

"Not a poet. You may have one more guess."

"I'm afraid you will have to enlighten me. I cannot think who it might be."

"It is Lord Howell!" Her body trilled with glee as she said the words, for the viscount did indeed admire her work, and the knowledge mattered a great deal to her.

"Well, now, that is a thing, indeed!" Her father sat back, his hands paused in mid-action. "To have gained his lordship's attention is no small achievement. What does his letter say?"

"I shall read it to you." She reached into her dress pocket and drew out the page, unfolding it with reverence.

"'*To the poet, Miss Sophia Grant.*'" Sophia grinned up at her father. "It is official. Our most prominent member of society has declared me a poet."

"And so he should. I am gratified to discover that he is the man of good taste I had always thought him to be."

They shared a moment of happy connection. Then Sophia read on.

"'*I am pleased to say that I acquired your volume of poems for my library at Munro House. I fully intend to recommend it to my circle of close friends. They will, no doubt, do the same. In fact, I imagine a reprint will become necessary to accommodate the growing interest.*'"

"I shall write to the printers after breakfast," Mr. Grant promised. "How many copies shall I order?"

"It might be a fair number," Sophia explained. "His lordship has an idea in mind. He is quite the champion to our cause."

"Is he? That is very generous of him. You are lucky indeed to have such a busy man turn his thoughts to your advancement."

For a moment, Sophia imagined a flicker of suspicion in her father's eyes. Could he possibly think Lord Howell would be interested in her for anything beyond poetry? Her thoughts drifted down to her imperfect legs, and the illness that had wrought them so. No, her father had nothing to fear. No viscount would want her for a bride. However, Lord Howell had obviously given her condition some thought. She voiced as much to her father.

"He even considers the difficulty of my physical situation in the event he has planned."

"Event? What event?" The first tendril of opposition curled into the conversation.

"See for yourself." Sophia, too anxious to read the words

aloud, thrust the letter at her father.

He perused the contents, lifting his head after a few lines to ask, "A poetry reading? He cannot possibly expect you to travel to that mausoleum of a house. You will catch your death of cold, even if every fire in every hearth were lit!"

"Read on," she urged. "He has taken that into account."

Mr. Grant grumbled under his breath but finished the letter. "I see," he remarked, though he frowned as he said it. "He suggests we host it here. He will be in attendance. And he will advertise this formal gathering among his learned associates. Exactly how many people are we talking about, Sophia?"

"I believe, not counting the household, one might expect at least…thirty?"

"Thirty strangers in my house!"

"Thirty *supporters*, Papa. It is only for the afternoon. And his lordship will be here. From what I understand, he is no more an enthusiast of such gatherings than we are. And yet he will do this for me, whom he does not even know beyond what I have written. Can *you* bear it, Papa, for me, your daughter?"

A multitude of emotions flitted across her father's face. Sophia dug her nails into her palms. She had played the only two cards she had. Her father was as great a friend to her career as he was an enemy of her freedom. Having denied her the one, he would be hard-pressed to deny the other as well. As for the viscount, he was a difficult man to say *no* to. If his presence necessitated the attendance of countless others… Well, it would be a close call.

"We…We could arrange it for a Monday. Then you would not have to endure it." It was a last, desperate attempt to convince her father. Her fingers dug deeper into her palms. And then…

"Don't be ridiculous! Of course I will be there. What sort of father do you think I am?"

Sophia was so elated at his response that it was easy to ignore his question. She flung her arms around his shoulders, almost toppling from her chair as she did so.

"Oh, thank you, Papa! Thank you! A thousand times thank you! You have no idea how much this means to me."

Her father stood and carefully settled her back in her seat. "It would be impossible not to know," he said matter-of-factly. "You have nearly thrown yourself upon the floor with enthusiasm. Sometimes I wonder if you are so very different to Adr—"

He cut himself off. The air filled with unspoken thoughts.

"Papa…" Sophia reached her hand across to his arm. He ignored it, sitting down and returning his attention to his crumpet.

"I assume his lordship will only invite the sort of people with whom he would be willing to spend time," he said stiffly. "I will not stand to be a curiosity for idle gossip."

"No, Papa." Dread descended upon her at the thought of Miss Sangford. Surely, she would be on her best behavior if she hoped to snag the earl? Sophia had no choice but to hope it was so.

"Two weeks," her father pondered aloud. "It seems a little rushed. Then again, I imagine the viscount has few openings in his schedule."

"Cook need only prepare some light refreshment," Sophia reassured him. "It should not place any undue pressure on her. And no one is spending the night, so there is little to be done by way of readying rooms. Honestly, Papa, now that I know it is really happening, I am grateful it will be soon. I already feel my nerves beginning to tremble."

Turning to face her, her father cupped her hand in his. Sophia looked at the protective fingers curled around her own, then up into his eyes. They were filled with such compassion that she had to look away. He really did love her. And yet…

One day, she would have to stand her ground. Tell him what the darker side of his love—his ferocious attachment—was doing to the family. Today, she had been a little brave. But it would take far more courage to broach the topic of marriage.

At least Miss Sangford could be held at bay a while longer.

Two more Mondays with Tobias were granted her. Sophia bloomed at the thought. She felt the echo of his lips against her neck, a soft, lingering heat creeping into her cheeks.

"Are you all right?" her father asked. "You are looking a little flushed. If this gathering is going to cause you further strain, we shall call it off at once."

"No!" Sophia cried in alarm. "Er… I mean, there is no need for that. It is a little excitement, and nothing else. I will settle soon. After breakfast, I will select the poems for the reading. Once I have a task to focus on, the apprehension will fade."

Her father's worried gaze softened. "I suppose I should attend to my own duties also, most important of which is the letter to the printers. Once you have won the hearts of your audience at the reading, we must make sure they are not disappointed when they seek your book for themselves."

How ready her father was to give her up to her readers! How easily he spoke of hearts and passion when it came to her poems. A barrier of pages kept her safe from them, tucked away at home, hidden behind her words.

More and more, she felt dissatisfaction and resentment replace helplessness and acceptance. One day, she would…

Her house of cards collapsed. She would never have the strength to do what Adriana had done. It just wasn't in her.

However, when she imagined her future without Tobias, little whorls of courage rose up within her. It needed to percolate into a full-scale tornado before anything could be done to change her fate. That seemed a phenomenon unlikely in the climate of her life.

And yet, despite her doubts and fears, Sophia had a sense that the weather was shifting.

CHAPTER SIXTEEN

T HE ATMOSPHERE IN the Howell carriage was permeated with nervous tension. Each of the three men gave the impression that all was well, but the discerning observer would quickly have recognized it as a façade. Tobias certainly knew it was.

The owner of the luxurious coach was staring out of the window. Perhaps he was considering his escape. Perhaps he was surveying the land, noting improvements that might be made to his own estate. What he was purposefully *not* doing was thinking about the imminent gathering, where his untasted pies awaited him.

Tobias suppressed a giggle. He was not prone to giggling, but he was on edge, and the sound bubbled up inside of him like a hiccup. It was not dignified. He was urgently trying to get it under control before meeting Sophia's father. The last thing he needed was to shake the man's hand while grinning like a simpleton.

His uncle, bless his heart, bore the ordeal of imminent socializing with great fortitude. He was here for his friend, for an afternoon of excellent verse, and—if he could manage it—very little conversation, indeed. His countenance was the most convincingly stoic of the three gentlemen. Given his age, he had had the most practice at it. But his veneer was a little tarnished whenever Tobias addressed him, for his concentrated effort at calm would be interrupted, and he would barely be able to summon a meaningful response.

Unfortunately for him, Tobias found comfort in talking. The nearer they came to the Grant residence, the more Tobias nattered, and the more disconcerted his uncle became. This might have been yet another reason why the viscount kept his gaze aimed away from them, so as not to be drawn into their awkward duet.

"This is Sophia's favorite tree." Tobias resumed his running commentary as they turned into the drive. "She can see it from her window and watch the seasons change through it. Whether it be adorned with fresh, green shoots, filled with leaves and birdsong, or laden with snow, it is a constantly changing visage."

"I see."

"Do you, Uncle? I scarce think you turned your head. If you do so quickly, you might yet catch a glimpse of it. Ah, no, you have missed it. However, we can now see the flowerbed she instructed the gardener to plant. They are all her mother's favorite flowers. I recognize some that grow in your garden also."

"That is very likely."

"I suppose that is true. There are some species that are be-loved by all. Or it might be that these varieties grow best in the local soil. Which do you think it is?"

"I could not say."

Tobias stared at his uncle for a second. When no further communication was forthcoming, he proceeded to steer the conversation—such as it was—on his own.

"Look! Six, seven, *eight* carriages are here already! It is well that the Grants have such a long drive to accommodate them all. This bodes well for your selection, does it not, Lord Howell? So many fine pies…er, *ladies* to choose from."

At the sound of his name, the viscount dragged his mind away from its distraction.

"What was that?" he asked.

"I said, it seems a large number of families have accepted the invitation to the poetry reading. You will be quite surrounded by a crowd of beautiful women. And their chaperones, of course. How fortunate you are."

Both the viscount and the earl grew visibly glum at these words. Lord Howell, who had only just surfaced from his self-imposed silence, retreated to it hastily. Uncle Edward mirrored his distant stare, the view in their minds' eyes likely filled with anything *but* a bevy of beautiful young women. Tobias, by contrast, was delighted. A crowd meant cover from which to observe. And he wanted to observe their host. He intended to find the loophole through which Mr. Grant could be approached. A quiet corner from which to monitor Miss Sangford would be helpful too.

Fortunately, no such spying eyes were upon them as they pulled up to the entrance. They were able to make their arrival incognito, in so far as the insignia of the Howell family upon the carriage doors allowed.

Tobias almost forgot himself, ready to spring from the carriage, keen to channel his nervous energy into movement. But the footman bowed and said, "Mi'lord," before stepping back, reminding Tobias that there was a correct order to things. He fought against a bouncing knee, then fairly shot from the compartment when his turn finally came.

He immediately resumed his tide of conversation, notching up the rate of speech as they approached the heavy oak front doors. "I think you will like their library, Uncle, if we can persuade our host to let you view it. It is small compared to your own, but I believe very few families can boast a collection like yours, barring perhaps his lordship's here. The books here are not as old, but they have a wide range of classics in the original tongue, purchased, I am certain, to feed Miss Grant's hungry mind. She is quite fluent in Latin, Greek, French..."

"Yes, yes, dear boy," Lord Carthige interjected, "but may I suggest you rein in your enthusiasm somewhat? It will not take much to attract the watchful gaze of her father. You would do well to draw no attention to yourself. Let the afternoon be memorable for Miss Grant's verse, and not your verbosity."

"You are right, of course, Uncle. Thank you for your advice. I will make every effort to heed it. It would be a shame if I made a poor impression at the one opportunity I had to make a favorable one. Who knows when I might…"

"Tobias."

"Yes, Uncle?"

Lord Carthige held Tobias's gaze in patient silence.

"Oh. Oh, I see. Yes. Less talking. Indeed, that is for the best. I wonder if…" Tobias paused. "I'm still doing it, aren't I?" He dragged his fingers through his hair. "This is going to be harder than I thought."

Uncle Edmund patted him awkwardly on the shoulder. "Perhaps begin with silence. You will learn more from listening than speaking."

Tobias opened his mouth to express his agreement, saw his uncle's look of dismay, and closed it at once. He received a nod of approval as his reward.

In his newly wordless state, Tobias noticed Lord Howell pausing as the butler turned to show them in. He set his broad shoulders squarely, straightened to his full impressive height, and restored the bearing of Viscount Howell. To look at him, one would never guess how he dreaded entering those doors.

Tobias and his uncle planted themselves firmly behind him. It was an act of support, but also a reminder that his lordship's escape route was now cut off. To his credit, the viscount strode ahead into the home of the Grants with such convincing bravado, he seemed almost arrogant. Tobias would not have been surprised if people assumed he were. It would take a very special woman to peel away this outer layer without triggering his alter ego, the hapless suitor.

Uncle Edward had reverted to his perpetual discomfort in any space that did not surround him with books or art. The sound of many feminine voices rose up from a distant room. Tobias could have sworn he saw his uncle hitch in his step, as if there were a moment in which he had to persuade himself to keep moving forward.

All three of them slowed as they reached the doorway to a large reception room. The volume of chatter and sheer heat from a multitude of bodies so close together created a sort of barrier to be crossed upon entering.

They may have stood there indefinitely. Certainly, the viscount was in no hurry to proceed. Somewhere within the gathered throng, however, someone recognized him. News of his arrival passed from ear to ear, faces turning like dominoes toward the doorway. A body pushed forward—a man with hair so dark, it was almost black, tied back in a queue. His was not a friendly face, but his greeting was civil enough.

"Welcome, my lords." Their host gave a stiff, almost military bow."

Mr. Grant gave Tobias a fleeting scrutiny. However, being in the company of the viscount seemed to earn him instant approval. Tobias had his tongue under control, so that the opportunity for embarrassing himself was greatly diminished.

"My nephew," Lord Carthige explained. "Mr. Tobias Mannerly. He stays with me at Newcliffe Hall and assists in the unenviable task of cataloging my extensive library. He has a great admiration for Miss Grant's writing. In fact, it was he who brought it to my attention."

Mr. Grant reached out his hand and Tobias did the same. They shook like equals, though Tobias was convinced his fingers had turned to jelly. So far, he saw nothing of concern. Just because Mr. Grant was not a chatty sort of fellow did not make him a villain. Goodness, that would make his uncle and the viscount the worst of the lot!

"I must apologize for the humidity," said their host. "We cannot open the windows. There is a chill outside, which I must protect my daughter from. But I could offer you cold refreshment. And we have a well-aired parlor adjacent if you wish to have some relief."

Lord Howell must have longed for the solitude of that parlor, but all eyes in the room were now upon him. "Thank you, Mr. Grant," he said with a convincing smoothness. "I am most grateful that you agreed to play host in my stead. Your daughter's health was the very reason I suggested it. It is right that you put her needs first. We will manage nicely."

Mr. Grant bowed again. "Thank you for your understanding. Not everyone has been as…agreeable."

"Ladies are more delicate," the viscount explained, as if he had knowledge on the subject. "We must allow for their lack of durability."

Tobias felt laughter gurgling to the surface. The viscount really was trying his best. Only, his best involved viewing women as some sort of engine, to be maintained rather than cherished. Tobias could only hope that, among the ladies present, they might find someone who didn't mind.

"Fortunately," Mr. Grant responded with absolute earnest, "we have several gentlemen present too, should our feminine company feel the need to faint. I do not think my footmen alone could deal with this much *delicacy*."

"They do appear armed with fans," the viscount noted.

"Will we be seated soon?" Lord Carthige asked. "The ladies should be much more comfortable when not exerting them-selves."

Tobias rolled his eyes inwardly. What was the matter with the members of his sex? Was he the only one who saw women as strong, fascinating beings who were as resilient as any man? Heaven help all the eligible young ladies here if this was what they had to put up with. His own parents had set a very different example. His sister had not been raised to think herself dainty or insufficient in any way. She was an accomplished woman, excellent at both needlework and horsemanship. He, in turn, had been taught to expect such qualities in his choice of wife. Sophia might not be able to ride, but—by gum!—she was by no means weak. Anyone who could survive her losses and limitations—and flourish in spite of them—was made of strong stuff.

He took stock of his host. Mr. Grant did not appear particularly cruel. There was no hardness to his features, save for the absence of any mirth. In fact, his eyes were those of a man with deep feeling. There was something familiar about his manner. A sense of tight control over self. As though it were necessary to survive. The way a mountain gripped the earth when it felt the magma shift below. It was like...yes, like the way his uncle projected peace onto his person, without necessarily feeling it. Tobias had always assumed it was because people made Uncle Edmund uncomfortable. Was it something from his childhood? Tobias did not know, but it saddened him to think that his beloved uncle should carry an injury in the way Mr. Grant did.

Mr. Grant, meanwhile, had cast his gaze over the room, as if performing an informal census. "We are waiting for one or two more guests before we begin. I am sorry I cannot introduce my sons to you. Henry has returned to his studies at Cambridge, and George was called away on a business matter. They are very disappointed to miss their sister's debut, but needs must. Perhaps you will allow me to introduce my daughter to you in the meantime? She has already been settled in readiness for the reading."

"It would be an honor to finally meet the talented young lady," Lord Howell answered. "I am certain my companions are equally as eager to do so."

He followed his host and companions obediently across the room. The conversation among the other guests had resumed, but at a lower pitch, as each person tried to hear what Lord Howell was saying over their own pretense at chatter.

At last, they reached the small dais that had been erected to face the chairs so that the audience might see Sophia clearly, since she was seated too. Tobias could only imagine how such focused attention horrified her. Indeed, she was clearly relieved to see him approach. Her pinched expression relaxed at once, a warm smile easing onto her features.

"Lord Howell," her father began, "my eldest daughter, Miss Sophia Grant."

"A pleasure to make your acquaintance," he replied. "Thank you for being willing to share your work with us."

Sophia lowered her head by way of a curtsey. Then her eyes flicked up and she brought her hand to her heart. "It is a privilege, sir."

Next, her father indicated the earl. "I don't know if you recognize Lord Carthige. We had him to dinner when you were just a girl. I should say your mother had him to dinner. As I'm sure everyone knows, I have always preferred to be a private man."

"That is precisely why I remember you, my lord," Sophia added. "Guests here are a rarity and therefore always make an impression on me."

Lord Carthige offered a wry smile. "I am grateful to be remembered. Not that I deserve it. I have been equally remiss with my dinner invitations."

"Do not worry yourself, my lord. I would have been unable to attend them. You are quite safe from us in your seclusion."

"I am no longer as cut off from society as I once was, Miss Grant." He indicated to Tobias. "My nephew, Mr. Tobias Mannerly, has kindly provided me with his company and a shared love of books."

To Tobias's complete and utter astonishment, his uncle leaned in a bit closer to Sophia and took on a tone that was both conspiratorial and teasing. "What I had not counted on, is his equal love for conversation. I do not mind a critique on the volumes we are cataloguing, but Mr. Mannerly enjoys a lively debate on a much wider range of topics. I am unused to it. And yet, it is not entirely unpleasant. However, today, with so many people in attendance, he might have his fill. Perhaps, if we can exhaust him, I will be spared this evening."

And then, to Tobias's horror and delight, his uncle winked at Sophia. *Winked.* Edmund Stopford, Earl of Carthige, notorious hermit and shunner of fellow humans, had *winked* at a young woman.

Sophia laughed and clapped her hands. "You have my sympathies, Lord Carthige! It sounds absolutely terrible. But I will say you bear it bravely."

At these words, the earl straightened up. "Well now, Nephew, the lady has been warned. Do your worst."

Sophia turned her dancing eyes upon Tobias. And he found he had absolutely nothing to say.

There was much he *wanted* to say. How wonderful it was to see her without meeting in secret. How she looked radiant, as always. How his uncle was full of surprises. He racked his brain for something he might be permitted to say aloud. Embarrassingly, he came up with very little except, "I am a great admirer, Miss Grant. Of your works, I mean. I am thankful my uncle's invitation was extended to include me."

"Thank you, Mr. Mannerly. I wonder—since you are so well-read, and more willing to express those opinions, as your uncle has indicated—whether you would look over my list of poems I have chosen for the reading? My father professes to love them all equally, which is impossible and also unhelpful. I do not wish to disappoint our guests. Will you speak honestly and tell me whether I have chosen well?"

"It would be my honor," Tobias replied. "Though I might be in agreement with Mr. Grant."

"I shall be very disappointed if you are," Sophia warned. Then, as her father turned away to continue the introductions of the other guests to the viscount, she whispered, "She's not here."

Tobias was startled by the unexpected comment. "Who?"

"Miss Sangford. I sent her the invitation and she accepted. All a bit of a farce, really, since she demanded it in the first place. And now she's not here."

Tobias surveyed the room. There were a few taller ladies present, but none with the distinctive spindly limbs and pinched expression. He was not surprised. The other guests had been handpicked. Miss Sangford would most assuredly not have been on the viscount's list. "She probably wants to make a grand entrance," he told Sophia. "You know, arrive at the last minute so all heads will turn to acknowledge her. There really wouldn't be any other way for my uncle to take note of her."

"What if she doesn't come?" Sophia fretted. "What if something has prevented her? Will she still keep our secret? I have no other plan if this one fails."

"Miss Sangford would not miss this opportunity to further her own cause. She would neglect her closest friend's wedding if it meant arranging her own. Not that she stands a chance."

"I hope you're right. I don't know what unsettles me more: worrying about her being here or worrying about her not being here."

"I don't think you have a choice anymore," Tobias remarked, straightening up. "Look who has come to try her luck at fishing for a husband."

CHAPTER SEVENTEEN

E VEN FROM HER seated position on the far side of the room, Sophia could make out the unmistakable figure of Miss Irene Sangford. Their adversary had gone to a lot of trouble to make herself appealing. She certainly was very clever. Instead of feathers and gem-studded silver, which were favored by young women keen to show off their wealth, Miss Sangford had chosen a single velvet ribbon at her neck. It was simple and elegant, designed to attract a very particular sort of man to whom money was irrelevant.

Her dress, too, was classical rather than ostentatious. It suggested taste. This, the ensemble told the observer, was a woman of quality. She was not here to impress, but to quietly sip from the cup of culture. Sophia had to hand it to her. She was no amateur.

In keeping with her pretense, Miss Sangford ignored the eligible gentlemen present and made a beeline for Sophia. She pasted an expression of pure joy upon her face as she approached, and said, a little too loudly, "Miss Grant! Thank you *so* much for the invitation. I was meant to be away in Steeples with my family. But when I heard you were doing a reading of your poems, I simply had to come! My parents have generously delayed their travels until next week so that I might attend."

It was such an outrageous lie that Sophia momentarily forgot the risk of calling her out on it.

"Did your parents not wish to join us, since such sacrifice was made to be here?" she inquired.

Miss Sangford's smile froze. It was discarded in favor of a slow, sad shake of the head. "Alas, my mother is fatigued from all the arrangements that have been made. And my father never attends a social gathering without her. They are very devoted to each other, you know. I can only hope to have a marriage half as happy as theirs."

Unable to fake a modest blush, she opted for tilting her fan coyly at her face, as if hiding the non-existent surge of color in her face.

Sophia was both disgusted and impressed. The woman was a master actress, albeit one with no scruples. If Lord Carthige hadn't been a confirmed bachelor, he would have been easy prey.

Fanning herself languidly, Miss Sangford cast her eyes upon the other guests and pretended to notice the earl for the first time.

"Ah, I see your neighbor is in attendance. What noble friends you have, Miss Grant. I wonder if it would be possible to be introduced to him? I believe we have mutual interests."

Now that the moment had come, Sophia was very unwilling to see it through. But a bargain had been struck. There was no way around it.

"I shall ask his nephew to do the honors," she said grudgingly, "as I am unable to leave my seat without exerting myself. You remember Mr. Mannerly, I hope?"

Miss Sangford looked Tobias up and down, settling at last on a look of happy surprise. "Ah, yes, I thought you looked familiar. Help me, if you will. Where was it we met before?"

Sophia wished she could kick their tormentor in the shins and get away with it. The vixen could do with a good thrashing. How she slept at night with all the mischief she plotted by day was beyond Sophia's extensive imagination. *Humph!* In all likelihood, she slept like a baby, having no moral compass to burden her thoughts.

If his rigid body language was any indication, Tobias was equally appalled by Miss Sangford's question. He glared at her, clenching his jaw before answering.

"I believe it was at church."

"So it was! A wedding, if I recall. Although for the moment, I cannot quite put my finger on whose wedding it was."

The warning shot had been fired.

Tobias heeded it, balling his fists at the manipulation, then releasing them helplessly. "This way, if you please." He gestured. "My uncle is over there, standing beside Lord Howell."

Sophia hated having to see him beholden unto a person of such low character. It grieved her that the reason he was bound thus was to protect her. She saw Miss Sangford's face fill with triumph as she lifted it toward her target, her eyes gleaming, her lips pouting. And then Sophia watched that triumph drain away.

"The viscount is with him." Miss Sangford did not seem pleased. But, then again, when was she ever pleased unless she was plotting mischief?

"Yes," Tobias said, "they are friends."

"You did not tell me this."

Was that an edge of panic in her voice? Miss Sangford kept her gaze focused rigidly on the viscount, not stirring a muscle, rather like a doe who hoped the hunter would not notice her before he moved on. Sophia grimaced at the thought. Miss Sangford was no gentle-eyed doe.

"Why would I mention their friendship?" Tobias enquired. "What relevance did it have to our arrangement? You demanded to meet Lord Carthige. We have complied. What does it matter whether Lord Howell attends also?"

"You must separate them."

Sophia, watching the scene unfold between Tobias and his nemesis, drew a delicious conclusion. She declared it with relish. "Lord Howell knows you! Well enough not to like you! You're afraid he'll reveal your wiles to the earl."

"Hush!" Miss Sangford bit back in a low voice. "People will

hear you. You don't want your secrets exposed any more than I do."

"What would you have us do?" Tobias asked. "I have no excuse to call Lord Howell away. You are going to have to put on your best façade and hope his lordship believes you are a changed woman."

"That man," Miss Sangford said through grinding teeth, "is a buffoon. For all his money and fine breeding, he wouldn't know a good woman if she sat right on his lap!"

"Tried it, have you?" Sophia couldn't help herself. There was nothing in their agreement that said she had to be polite.

Her enemy gave her a withering glare.

"It would be amusing if my uncle were to look this way at this exact moment," said Tobias.

They waited as Miss Sangford struggled to swallow her rage, attempt a smile, and fail miserably. The result was a rather frightening rictus, which Sophia would have loved for Lord Carthige to see.

"I'll show you *amusing*," Miss Sangford said, her lips tight with the effort at smiling. "You get Lord Howell away from the earl, or I leave now and start writing a detailed letter to our host. I might even add a few trimmings if I let my imagination go."

When Tobias did not move, she added, "Now, if you please."

He looked helplessly at Sophia. She had no idea what to do. Her nerves were already strained with the public attention on her. Miss Sangford's threat pushed her up against a wall. Her brief satisfaction at seeing her enemy writhe was spent. All that remained was fear. Her heart began to race. Her throat was closing. She looked for Katie, her wide eyes signaling for help. Katie materialized in an instant, grabbing an aromatic pouch from her mistress's reticule and holding it firmly beneath her nose.

"Don't... let... my father... see," Sophia panted between gulps of breath.

Tobias shifted to block her from view. "Use your fan," he instructed Miss Sangford. She remained motionless, except for a look of disdain that spread across her features. "Look," he urged, "if Mr. Grant thinks she cannot manage, he will send everyone home. That includes you and my uncle. Now, use your fan!"

The reluctant small breeze offered Sophia some relief from the stifling heat in the room. The fact that Miss Sangford was forced to help revive her offered relief of a different kind. Her heart slowed. The tension ebbed. Her breathing eased. Her thoughts cleared. In fact, this uncomfortable episode had given her exactly the inspiration she needed.

"Take…your uncle…to the library," she told Tobias, gradually gaining sufficient breath to do so. "You know where it is. There is still time…before the reading. I will tell my father I wish to rest a while before we start. The library is but two doors down. It is warm, but empty. My father will accept my being moved there. I have greeted enough people. He will likely want to stay at my side, but Miss Sangford could do a little show of concern and come with me instead. Introductions can be made there while my father tends to the viscount. Are we in accord?"

"It's worth a try," Tobias agreed. "Do you think you can feign concern, Miss Sangford?"

She appeared immune to his slight, lowering her lashes and speaking in an even tone. "You fetch Lord Carthige, and I will manage my part quite nicely. Just make sure he doesn't bring his friend along to the library. How you do that is up to you."

Tobias gave a glance of despair to Sophia, his brow furrowed, his mouth slack. He was not, by nature, devious. He had not lived a life like hers that required it. She nodded at him with encouragement.

"Just remind his lordship why he is here," she coaxed.

It was a subtle enough clue to go right over the head of Miss Sangford. But Tobias would understand. He set off across the room, shoulders squared.

He approached his uncle, turned to indicate Sophia, and then gestured toward the library. A short discussion ensued, then agreement. Tobias and Lord Carthige began to make their way across the crowded room. When the viscount made to join them, Tobias stopped. He lowered his head, then tilted it slightly in reference to the other guests. Lord Howell's cheeks became touched with color. He appeared quite deflated. What must have been words of encouragement followed. Sophia could not read lips, but she could have sworn the earl said, "Chin up, old boy." At which point there was a sigh and a look of resignation. The viscount resumed his confident air, though it demanded no small effort. Mere seconds after his companions left without him, the wretched soul was surrounded by mothers, eager to introduce their daughters.

"Foolish things," Miss Sangford sneered. "They're welcome to him. You wouldn't catch me fawning over him like that."

"Is that because you've already had your turn?" Sophia asked sweetly.

Miss Sangford looked down at Sophia from her considerable height, made more so by the fact that Sophia was sitting down.

"If I'm going to marry for money and status, I prefer an older man. There wouldn't be as many years to put up with him before the poor dear was off to the Elysian Fields. I think I am rather well suited for the role of dowager countess, don't you think?"

Sophia's blood boiled at such callous words. She felt her cheeks glow with revulsion.

"Goodness, are you feeling unwell?" Miss Sangford asked, slipping smoothly into her mask. "I shall ask your father to come at once."

"Don't overdo it," Sophia warned. "We want him to let me rest in the library, not be spirited away to my room and the event canceled."

Miss Sangford waved her fingers over her shoulder as she glided through the cluster of bodies to reach Mr. Grant. Seconds later, he was hurrying toward Sophia. There was just enough time for Lord Howell to catch a glimpse of Miss Sangford and frown.

"What's the matter?" Mr. Grant asked, his forehead pleated with worry.

"Nothing, Papa. It's just so hot and stuffy. I was thinking to sit in the library a while. I've greeted everybody, and there is still time before my reading starts. I would just like to catch my breath."

Her father considered this. "You would tell me if it was all too much for you, wouldn't you? I know how much this means to you. But you must not put your health at risk."

"I promise, Papa. A half hour in the library is exactly what I need. I can go through my poems in private, without the eyes of our guests upon me."

"Very well. Katie must stay with you. I will check on you as often as I can."

Seizing the moment, Miss Sangford inserted herself into his line of sight, dripping with honeyed tones. "I could avail myself to Miss Grant, if you would permit me. I am content to browse your collection as long as she fares well. If something were amiss, I would be right there and could support her while young Katie finds you."

"That is very kind, Miss…"

"Sangford. Descended from the Hanover *Sanfords*. You may have heard of us." She raised her fan coyly. "Of course, we don't speak of it often, but it has been suggested we are distant cousins to Her Majesty."

"Suggested by whom?" Sophia asked before she could stop herself.

"I'm sure I don't know," Miss Sangford replied, looking down at Sophia over the frill of her fan. "One does not like to ask such indelicate questions."

Mr. Grant cleared his throat. "Yes, well, thank you for your kind offer, Miss Sangford. I would be most grateful for my Sophia to have a companion of good standing while she rests. You will certainly be able to provide more depth of conversation than Katie. She attends well to her mistress, but I often wonder if my daughter does not want for more refined company."

"Katie has always been more than sufficient, Papa," Sophia retorted. "She may not be an aficionado of poetry, but that's what

I have my many correspondents for."

"You have always borne it well," her father answered sadly. "But the absence of your mother robs you of a woman's comfort."

"I was under the impression you have sisters, Miss Grant," purred Miss Sangford. "That must surely be some consolation to you. Perhaps you might introduce us and we could visit with you together in the library."

"Bess is not yet out in society," replied Sophia, burying the urge to thump the woman with her volume of poems. It would be the highest form of poetic justice she could deliver. "And Adriana is…away." She glanced at her father. His ears were burning, but he remained silent. Of course he would. Unless he was forcibly reminded of her, Adriana did not exist.

"Father, I will need a footman," she hinted, though really she just wanted him as far away from Miss Sangford—descendant of the Hanover *Sanfords*—as possible.

"I will have one sent to you. And I will look in on you presently." He touched his forelock to his guest, who lowered her eyes demurely.

The moment he left, Sophia hissed at Miss Sangford, "What are you playing at? My father is a suspicious man. Do not goad him. You will undo your own scheme. And us along with it."

A smug response formed on Miss Sangford's lips, but it summarily dissolved when the footman approached. He lifted Sophia in a smooth, practiced motion. She placed her arms around his neck—an action that should have felt intimate, tender, but never did. It was done merely to steady herself, an attempt to maintain a bearing of dignity in an undignified position. What he felt, she could not say. Perhaps it was simply a task to be completed. Maybe, like Katie, he performed his duty with an added sense of kindness and loyalty.

Regardless of his motives, he transported Sophia carefully to the library, a minor hero in her story, while her adversary followed like an ominous shadow.

CHAPTER EIGHTEEN

SOPHIA WAS GENTLY deposited on the library's sunny window sofa. Katie took up a protective position at her right shoulder, squaring off against Miss Sangford, who had followed close behind. Upon their arrival, two gentlemen seated nearby, bent in concentration over a scattering of yellowed pages, lifted their heads in unison.

"Oh, Lord Carthige, Mr. Mannerly, I see you have found my mother's sketches." Sophia smiled as she made herself comfortable on the plush, burgundy upholstery. "They are rather good, aren't they? She had such an eye for detail. You should see her watercolors. Unfortunatcly, they are upstairs. They really were too lovely to hide in a dusty, leather binding. Father had them framed and they hang in and around our various bedrooms. I could have the footman fetch one, if you like."

"That will not be necessary," the earl assured her, rising from his chair. "With your permission, we shall take our leave. You will have come here for a modicum of privacy, and we shall not disturb you."

Sophia cast an anxious glance toward Miss Sangford.

"Please do not leave on my account," she replied hastily. "I only seek relief from the press of bodies and the closeness their multitude of breaths create. There is room enough here for us to share without repeating those conditions."

"You are certain?" he asked.

"I am. Perhaps now you will reconsider my offer to show you one of my mother's paintings?"

"May I support Miss Grant's suggestion?" came the even tones of Miss Sangford. "I should very much like to see her mother's artistic skill."

The sincerity in her voice was so convincing, Sophia wondered if it could be real. Miss Sangford put so much effort into her pretense at warmth, it was strange that she should not choose to embrace it as an authentic part of herself. It would have made her search for a husband easier. And she would not have been the outcast in good society that she was. True friendship must have surely escaped her. Those who sought her company were no better than herself. They gave her no motive for improvement. Sophia found herself feeling a little sad for Miss Sangford. Until she remembered why she was here.

Lord Carthige, oblivious of Miss Sangford's motives, dipped his brow in acquiescence. "If the young lady is to be satisfied, then perhaps it is not such an imposition to have the painting sent for."

"Excellent!" Sophia turned to the footman, who had withdrawn to an inconspicuous position against the wall. "I think the portrait in the hallway outside George's room is a good choice. It is not Mama's best work, but it is still very fine. And it is an easy size to carry down the stairs."

The footman left at once, and Sophia caught Tobias's eye.

Now. It was time.

"I suppose," she said hurriedly, keen for the torment of this task to be over, "introductions are in order. My lord, may I introduce Miss Irene Sangford?"

"Sangford?" inquired the earl. "I am not familiar with your family." He turned to his nephew. "Was she on our list?"

"She came at my personal invitation, my lord," Sophia explained, while Miss Sangford stood like a horse whose pedigree was in question. "She is...er...that is to say...her family is descended from the Hanover Sanfords. A distant relation to the queen, I am told."

Why was she defending the woman? She despised her! But the idea of there being a list that one was not on brought out Sophia's protective instincts. She had too often been on such unwritten lists.

"Ah, yes." His lordship smiled, the mystery solved. "Are you a fellow connoisseur of poetry, Miss Sangford, or are you here simply to support a friend?"

To declare herself a friend would have been such an abomination of the truth that even Miss Sangford could not manage to say it. She spluttered a little as she formulated a response that was both suitable and attractive to her target. "Yes…well…if one is a friend to poetry, one must be a friend to Miss Grant. Her writing is most endearing."

"Is it?" Lord Carthige frowned. "That is not quite the word I had in mind. But then again, women see things differently. Which of her poems would be an example of this endearing quality? I would like to read it again with new eyes."

Sophia suppressed a grin. It was becoming clear that, while Miss Sangford had come prepared to charm the earl, she had not, in fact, researched the materials with which to charm him. It was amusing to watch the machine of her mind slip gears behind her startled eyes.

"I would far rather hear your thoughts on the matter, my lord," Miss Sangford deflected. "Your wealth of experience makes your opinion far more worthy."

"I disagree. It simply means I have had more opportunity to become set in my ways. The eyes of youth see with freshness, and a passion that we of an earlier generation have set aside. Yet I am willing to be enlightened."

"This ought to be good," Katie mumbled just near enough to Sophia's ear for her to hear. Sophia flicked her fan open to hide the smile that her lips could not.

"I confess, my memory is not reliable," said the floundering Miss Sangford. "Perhaps, if I had Miss Grant's book with me, I could find the lines I had in mind."

"I have a copy right here," Sophia announced, holding out the volume that she had placed on the seat beside her.

"Oh, good," Miss Sangford answered weakly. "Er...I might take a while to find the exact page. If you will be patient."

"Of course," replied his lordship. "Do not feel rushed on my account."

Miss Sangford, who was likely reading the poems for the first time, scoured the stanzas for anything that might qualify as endearing. She was probably kicking herself for choosing that descriptor. She would soon realize the book in her hands would offer her no evidence of such a quality. Passion, yes. Depth, yes. A rendering of classical images and thoughts, certainly. But the trite view that the work was endearing, like a child's misspelled letter to a favorite aunt, was quite misplaced.

As she turned the pages, Miss Sangford must have come to this very conclusion. Sophia imagined that she had, in all likelihood, stopped reading and was using the time with her head bowed over the book to scheme her way out of this situation.

Miss Sangford was spared further embarrassment when the footman arrived with the painting. Visibly relieved, she handed the book back to Sophia. "I shall find the poem later, if you like. Seeing your mother's art is a privilege I would not want to miss."

She reached for the frame and gazed at its contents thoughtfully. "It is very good," she said, in a voice that was strangely quiet. As if the portrait truly moved her. As if she meant what she said.

She turned to Lord Carthige. "Do you see, my lord?" She angled the painting so that he must stand close beside her to share its view. "It captures something that has since been lost."

The earl stood, almost shoulder to shoulder with the most dangerous person in the room, focused intently on the object before him, unaware of the peril he was in. "Ah, yes." He nodded. "Mr. Grant." He paused. "It is the way a wife sees her husband. All his complexity. Yet none of those many layers hide the essence of what he expresses through his eyes, and which she has captured through her brush."

"Love," Miss Sangford breathed.

"Indeed," the earl agreed.

There was an intake of breath throughout the room. Lord Carthige and Miss Sangford remained lost in the portrait. An unlikely pair to be captivated by such deep feeling. Neither mentioned the angle of the brushstrokes, or the subtlety of color. The artist had drawn them past mere technique into a well of emotion.

Just when Sophia felt she must say something, anything, to break the spell, her father entered the room and did it for her.

"I see all is well," he remarked, though Sophia did not currently share his sentiment. Miss Sangford and the earl lifted their heads reluctantly to behold the very man whose visage had held their attention a moment before.

"What do you have there?" Mr. Grant asked as he approached. He took the frame from Miss Sangford's unresisting hands, turning it to face him. He looked up at Sophia. "You had this fetched."

Sophia nodded. "Lord Carthige found Mama's portfolio of old sketches among our shelves. But they don't do her artistry justice, do they, Papa? Her paintings are a far better reflection of her talent."

Her father viewed the portrait once more. Sophia knew he did not see his own image. He was remembering the hours he'd posed for his wife. The way she'd looked at him while she'd worked. The things she'd seen in him that no one else had.

"She was a remarkable painter," Lord Carthige said quietly.

"She was a remarkable woman," Sophia's father replied.

"After all these years, it still cuts deeply," the earl said, as if to himself.

"You understand."

"You know I do."

Sophia's father lowered the painting, looking directly at his neighbor. "I had forgotten. It was remiss of me. Sometimes one's own sorrow blinds one to that of others."

"It was such a long time ago."

"Time changes nothing."

If only Miss Sangford had remained quiet.

But she didn't.

"Perhaps," she said, as one who could never understand such loss, "it is not time one needs, but the love of a good woman." She smiled her encouragement to the earl, testing his readiness to be pursued. The smile was not returned.

Sophia watched Lord Carthige's shoulders sag with weariness, while her father's expression morphed into searing contempt.

"I have already had the love of a good woman," he bit back. "Do you think I will ever find her equal?" He threw his hand out to indicate the earl, his voice rising with hurt and anger. "Are men like us supposed to tear the scars from our hearts so that some other woman who could never take her place can climb inside and nest there like a Gorgon?"

"Papa!" Sophia felt the tears welling up, the agony of her father too much to bear.

He whirled round to face her, his face a storm, his lips wet with spittle. She held his eyes, pleading silently. Within a few raggedy breaths, he had subsided. In two steps he was with her, taking her hand and lifting it to his bowed temple.

"Ah, no need for a Gorgon, my dear," he said, his voice low and thick. "My heart is already a stone." He leaned her knuckles onto his brow, his words now a mere whisper. "And you bear the weight of it."

Sophia's free hand reached up and cupped her father's cheek. "We all struggle together," she said. "Mama's absence is a wound that will not close."

Silence descended upon the room. No one knew what more to say. For once, that included Miss Sangford.

Sophia's father pulled her hand from his cheek, squeezed it

gently, and released it. The other he kissed and returned to her before taking a deep breath and turning to face his stunned audience. Remnants of recent emotion, mixed with embarrassment, showed upon his face.

If only she knew how to undo all that had just transpired! It was her fault, bringing strangers into his home, his sanctuary. He would have been spared this pain and humiliation, if not for Miss Sangford. And Sophia was the one who had given the enemy power over her with the secrets she kept from her father.

Then again, said a new voice inside her, bold and challenging, *was it not your father who forced such secrets upon you? Is it not he whose relentless sorrow extends all of ours? How long must we be held ransom to his misery? Why may his children not know the depth of love that he still feels?* Her pity shrank as this voice grew louder. How they all pandered to his needs! Fifteen years had not been enough for him to feel relief, nor offer it to his children.

She looked at Tobias, whose skin was flushed with silent restraint. Did he understand at last? Would he give up now, knowing there was no hope for her father to release her? Or did he wish, more than ever, to free her from this house of endless mourning?

She cursed her legs that could not stride from the room, could not offer her escape. She wanted to be far from her father and his morbid obsession with a memory. Instead, she would have to ask. *Please carry me. Please release me.* She felt a scream of frustration build in her throat.

Her father, by contrast, had calmed. "I fear I have rather shocked you," he said to Miss Sangford. "I pray you will forgive my outburst, for my daughter's sake."

Ah, thought Sophia, *Miss Sangford will do no such thing. She has seen that the earl is beyond her reach, beyond the reach of any woman. She need spare no one now. There's no reward in it for her.*

And yet, Miss Irene Sangford paused. Perhaps she remembered the room beyond was filled with men as well as women. Some would be fathers. But others might include an unwed brother, or chaperoning cousin. And if the earl and his friend the viscount were here, the other gentlemen would no doubt be from families of the highest caliber. To antagonize her host would be to cut off all potential that lay but two doors down.

"I have not yet heard Miss Grant read," she said at last. "Nothing has occurred that would prevent me from doing so. That is why we are here, after all."

Sophia's father bowed his head briefly. "Thank you for your understanding. It is most generous of you."

Lord Carthige tapped the back of his hand against Tobias's arm but addressed their host. "I believe your daughter came here to rest. We have robbed her of that. Please excuse us. My nephew and I will rejoin the others. Miss Sangford, may I escort you?"

He held out an arm and she took it readily. Even if her designs on the earl were a lost cause, being seen on his arm couldn't hurt.

So it was that when Lord Howell at last hastened into the library—most likely having had to fend off mothers and their eligible daughters—he found his friend in the clutches of the notorious Miss Irene Sangford.

"Miss Sangford," he cried, "I did not know you would be here."

It was the truth and a lie. She had definitely not been on his list of potential brides. He would not have expected her to attend the reading. But Sophia had seen him frown at Miss Sangford earlier. Her presence had been noted. Lord Howell knew she had followed them out of the room. Was that why he had come, clearly in a hurry, to join Lord Carthige?

Miss Sangford smiled her feral smile and leaned into her escort's arm more closely. "My lord, why would you concern yourself with whether I am here on not? I am no one of importance."

"So you know each other," Sophia's father interjected. "Well, that saves us the trouble of introductions."

"Indeed," Miss Sangford replied. "We often attend the same

events. We have several friends in common."

"Those are not my friends," the viscount replied gruffly. "There are functions I am expected to attend. That is all."

"Oh, you are too modest, Lord Howell," Miss Sangford said with practiced coyness. "All of Munro would be your friend. If you would but give them a chance."

"All of Munro can mind its own business," he huffed. "I know who my real friends are. And I have come to fetch one now. Carthige, if you would be so good, I need your assistance in a private matter. Mr. Mannerly, you would not mind escorting Miss Sangford instead."

It was not a request, and Tobias stepped forward at once to comply. The earl released Miss Sangford's arm with a polite bow of apology. Tobias grudgingly tipped his elbow toward her.

It was met with a look of disappointment, then disdain, and finally, inspiration. Miss Sangford threw a glance at Sophia, slipping her arm through that of Tobias and using her other hand to grip his bicep possessively. "You are too kind, sir. I could have managed well enough on my own, but this is very gentlemanly of you. I suppose I should be grateful you have no companion who might be jealous of your thoughtfulness toward me."

Sophia wanted to scratch her eyes out! Did she have to take *every* opportunity to sow malice? Sophia bit her tongue to keep from snapping at her. She would not give that hussy the satisfaction of knowing she had hit her mark.

Tobias, however, did not hold back. "I assure you, Miss Sangford," he said, while peeling her clutching hand from his person, "the sort of woman to whom I would form an attachment would not be envious of a simple act of chivalry. In fact, she would expect no less of me."

"Is that true, Miss Grant?" Irene Sangford asked innocently.

Sophia froze. "Why… Why do you ask me?"

"You are the only other genteel woman in the room. I will hardly ask the opinion of a lady's maid." She looked down the considerable length of her nose at Katie, then angled her neck toward Sophia. "Do you not agree the softer sex is easily made jealous?"

Sophia exhaled her relief, though the sudden fright she'd felt at the question still left her heart thrumming in her ears. "No," she said as firmly as her voice would let her, "we are no more inclined to such fits than the male of the species. It is a mark of an individual's insecurity, and not of their gender. Where one is loved well, there is no need to watch and worry."

"Well put, Miss Grant," said Lord Howell. And then, cutting off any further discussion on the matter, he declared, "Mr. Mannerly, I believe we were leaving. Shall we get on with it?"

In answer, Tobias began at once to step toward the door. Miss Sangford, who had twisted to face Sophia, was caught off-balance and fairly lurched forward upon his arm. He continued to walk, forcing her to rearrange her steps to match his. As soon as they passed the viscount, he fell in behind to flank them. Lord Carthige hesitated a moment, then followed them out the door.

"Well!" Sophia's father scratched the back of his neck. "They are an odd bunch. Miss Sangford seems not to know how to hold her tongue, though I am certain she means well. But she does have an unfortunate habit of raising ticklish subjects. A lapse in her education, no doubt. And then there is Lord Howell. A little arrogant, in my opinion. I suppose that a man of his station has not often been contradicted, and he has grown used to it. Yet when I observed him among our other guests, he appeared thoroughly uncomfortable. Is it the crowd, do you think? I could understand that. Not all men who are masters of their own domain enjoy the crush of so much humanity in one sitting. I certainly don't."

"They are opposites," Sophia replied. "Lord Howell commands an audience, and Miss Sangford repels them. Thank goodness Lord Carthige is such a gentle soul. For all his knowledge and wealth, he is unassuming and kind." Seizing the opportunity, she added, "One can see his nephew takes after him."

"Does he?" her father asked. "I can't say I noticed. He did not make much of an impression on me. A quiet chap. And accommodating. I suppose those are not bad qualities. But his uncle suggested he was a talkative sort of fellow. Perhaps I should be grateful he held his tongue. We did not need any further superficial chatter with Miss Sangford in the room. Self-control is a worthy quality to have. If he has inherited that from Lord Carthige, he has done well."

Sophia's heart rang out a happy and triumphant note to the heavens. A compliment! Her father had given Tobias a compliment! Granted, he would not have done so if he'd known the nature of the man's relationship with his daughter. But it was an honest view, and she hugged herself with the knowledge of it. Aloud, she merely said, "He does seem to be an honorable man. It must run in the family."

Her father snorted. "Insofar as it includes his uncle, Lord Carthige, yes. But the earl's brother is a dandy if ever I saw one. He wastes more money on his wardrobe than his wife does hers. Mr. Mannerly may be grateful if he resembles the older brother in character. In all likelihood, Lord Carthige wishes he could pass his title to his nephew rather than his brother. But that, I'm sorry to say, is not how these things work."

"It does not seem to bother Mr. Mannerly."

"No, indeed. But one cannot discount the benefits of a large inheritance."

"I imagine he only desires a sufficient income to supply his desire for books."

Her father nodded. "Another quality he shares with his uncle. Even today, among a crowd of eligible young women, one finds them both in the library."

Sophia felt the corners of her mouth twitch into a knowing smile.

"*Tch*, such a pity you were denied your rest for their sakes," her father said. Then he caught sight of her expression. "Yet you do not seem the worse for it."

"It was enough to breathe less stuffy air awhile," she answered. "And I was distracted from fretting about my reading."

"Do you feel ready to proceed, then? To be honest, I would be glad to have all these people out of my house at last."

Did she feel ready? Sophia considered this. She had survived Miss Sangford and all her devilry. There was nothing more they had to offer the woman, no fodder for her manipulations. The secrets she held over them could serve no further purpose. Thanks to the protection of the viscount, Lord Carthige had escaped unharmed. Miss Sangford might toy with the Grants of the world, but she would not risk the fury of nobility. Furthermore, Tobias and her father had met without incident. All in all, it had been as much of a success as she could have hoped for. What was a poetry reading when compared to challenges such as these?

"Yes," she declared, "I am as ready as I'll ever be. In fact, I am eager to get it over and done with before I change my mind."

Her father wasted no time. He sent the footman to return the painting, and then bring Sophia to her little dais. Meanwhile, Papa went on ahead to have the guests seated and ready to begin.

They were still milling about, selecting chairs next to their kin, or at least someone of suitable standing, when Sophia was carried in. Her presence sped up the procedure and mercifully kept many eyes from her for the moment. Those of Miss Sangford were still narrow with furious disappointment but were barely visible from her ostracized position near the back.

Sophia cast her gaze away from her audience and captured a tiny movement at the doorway. Familiar curls appeared around the partially opened door, followed by Bess's inquisitive eyes. They locked with Sophia's and a grin materialized on young Bess's face. Sophia tried not to react. Papa would not have been pleased to know that his youngest had snuck down to the gathering. Sophia wished that Bess, at least, might have been allowed to attend. The absence of her siblings at such a momentous occasion was sorely felt.

Bess's hand crept around the edge of the door to steady herself. Then another hand clasped it and, with a brief yelp, Bess disappeared. A worried frown from the housekeeper popped up instead. Sophia gave a quick, reassuring blink. Then the door closed once more. Sophia sighed her disappointment.

By now, the front row of seats had been filled. Sophia did not recognize many of the occupants. Squarely in the center, though, were her father, the viscount, the earl, and dear, precious Tobias. He made sure he had her attention. Sliding his hand surreptitiously to his chest, he pressed it to his heart, smiling encouragement at her.

Sophia focused on that hand, that smile. The noise in the room faded into the background. The silence that finally descended went unheeded by her, until her father stood and made an official statement of welcome. He turned and nodded for her to begin. Sophia barely acknowledged him. She opened her little volume of poems and lifted it so that her voice might travel better as she read. All the while, she felt the caress of Tobias's eyes upon her. The hours, days, weeks they had spent discussing her verse, in person and via countless letters, swirled around her like a mystical cocoon. She was safe. She was worthy. She was loved.

As she spoke her words to life, the rapt focus of a crowd of strangers was but a distant echo of her beloved's attention. For Sophia, it was a private conversation. For the hour that followed, she read her treasured works to an audience of one.

It was his face that stayed in her mind when Katie put her to bed that night. His applause that curled her toes with pleasure. And—she hugged herself with the thought—his lips she would seek when Monday brought him back again to her waiting arms.

CHAPTER NINETEEN

TOBIAS PUT DOWN the small pile of books he had rescued from the musty, old library. He and his uncle had just had tea and were ready to resume their task of reading and cataloging Newcliffe Hall's vast collection.

"Move that to the sideboard. There's a good fellow." Uncle Edmund gestured at the tray that held their empty cups and sandwich platter. "Let's not risk getting crumbs on our work."

Tobias did as he'd been instructed, then returned to the large desk they shared, sitting down opposite his uncle.

It had been two days since the poetry reading. Miss Sangford and her threats were a thing of the past. She had mercifully moved on. There had been no further communication from her. Some delicate inquiry told Tobias that the Sangfords had abruptly left for Steeples rather sooner than expected, a sure sign that their nemesis had fled with her tail between her legs. Sophia was safe. Their secret was safe. It was time to make a clean breast of things with his uncle. He had made a vow to do so, and he considered himself a man of his word. They must have honesty between them. Even if his uncle was disappointed in him. Even if it cost him his living, here among the books and the quiet conversation with a man he respected.

He had accepted the consequences when he had chosen to protect Sophia and their future together. But there was one repercussion that made this confession more difficult—it would hurt Uncle Edmund.

Across the desk sat a man who had been good to him. A singularly decent man. His only confidant beyond Sophia. Did he really have to break his heart? Would their friendship be able to recover from his deception?

There was only one way to find out.

"Uncle…" he began tentatively.

Uncle Edmund was checking the titles of the books Tobias had brought. "Are these the last volumes in the series? I have read two, and you, I believe, have managed three. I recollect there being ten volumes in this author's collection. But you have only brought a further three. What has become of the other two?"

"Perhaps your father never acquired the full set?" Tobias answered, momentarily put off his stride.

"More likely, he lit his pipe with the pages," his uncle muttered. "Very well, I suppose I shall have to write to my book agent and see if the missing volumes can be procured. There is something very unsettling about an incomplete collection."

"Er…before you do that, Uncle, there is something I need to talk to you about."

"Can it wait? We can talk over dinner."

"I really need to unburden myself to you. The longer I wait, the more difficult it becomes."

Uncle Edmund sat back, tapping his fingers lightly on the desk's mahogany surface. "Is this about Miss Grant again?"

"No. Well, yes, in a way."

"Well, which is it? Because honestly, Tobias, your mind has not been on your work of late. I count on you, you know. This library is too demanding a task for one man alone."

"You are right, of course." Tobias lowered his head. "I had hoped matters between myself and Miss Grant would have moved along rather more definitively. Yet an engagement remains elusive." He lifted his gaze quickly. "That is no excuse, mind you. I merely mean to indicate that my distractions should not interfere indefinitely."

"Hmm. And yet, here we are, conversing about Miss Grant once again when we should be applying ourselves to the books before us."

Tobias squirmed in his chair. "Sorry, Uncle. It's just that something has happened that forced my hand. It has meant I have had to keep a secret from you. And that does not sit well with me."

His uncle frowned. "You have not eloped, have you? I would be hard-pressed to approve of such behavior."

"No, Uncle, that is not our intention at all!"

"Good. Young people often have an exaggerated sense of the romantic. If it is not balanced with a solid dose of common sense, it rarely ends well."

"I will not apologize for loving Sophia as fully as I do," Tobias said rather more heatedly than he had intended to.

"Nor have I asked you to. Provided your sense of reason is not left in the wake of your other, more corporeal, senses."

Tobias subsided. His uncle was not asking anything more than his own parents would. For him to be a gentleman. To have integrity. *Ah, yes, about that...*

"I have used reason as far as circumstances allowed," he explained. "But it has not been enough to spare me a decision I deeply regretted having to make."

"Have you shamed your family?" his uncle asked sternly.

"Not directly. But I have betrayed a trust. And it is something I wish most earnestly to repair."

The earl leaned forward, steepling his fingers to his lips. "This sounds like a serious matter, Nephew. I can understand that it has taken your mind from our endeavor here."

"These are all reasons why I need to rid myself of the secret. And take accountability for my actions."

His uncle nodded sagely. "That is no less than I expect from you. Let's have it, then. I promise to listen and not judge unfairly."

Tobias groaned within. Why couldn't his uncle be more of a cad? He should shout his disappointment and beat his worthless nephew's back with a rod. That would be easier to bear. Instead, his uncle was breaking his heart with kindness.

He dipped his toe in the shallow end of the story, easing his uncle into the sordid details. "It has to do with the poetry reading," he began.

Uncle Edmund's pleasant demeanor shifted. "Does this matter affect the viscount? He is not only an important man, Tobias. He is my friend."

"No, not at all! The fact that Lord Howell had little to no success finding his match at that gathering had nothing to do with me!" He heard the defensiveness in his own voice and remembered where his guilt lay. "Er…however…the presence of Miss Sangford was my fault entirely."

"Miss Sangford?" The earl's brows knitted together. "What does she have to do with anything?"

The chair felt hard and uncomfortable. Tobias shifted his weight without relief. His skin grew hot and prickly. He needed to be rid of this secret! He sucked in his breath, then poured out the story all in a rush.

"She wanted to meet you, but she's a terrible person, all malice and manipulation. The very idea of her sidling up to you, let alone marriage! I shudder at the thought. I should've said *no*, but she wouldn't let me. She hasn't a virtuous bone in her body. She gave me no choice. And Sophia would have borne the brunt of it."

As Tobias hurtled toward the truth, he knew he was going about it with no sense of direction. He threw the facts out into the universe as the memories came to him. It was a haphazard course, and he could only hope his uncle would be able to make sense of it.

"Sophia's father would have found out," he stumbled on. "She was terrified. So we arranged for the poetry reading to throw her off. That is, Miss Sangford, not Sophia. I wouldn't want to be rid of Sophia. But you knew that. And I couldn't tell you, otherwise she—Miss Sangford—would write a letter filled with enough truth and added lies to destroy my chances."

He stopped, panting.

His uncle sat, stupefied, his mouth slightly open in a pose that was mildly undignified and utterly confused. Then he blinked and shook his head.

"I'm sorry. I didn't understand a word of that. I thought you and Miss Sangford were not previously acquainted. And what has she to do with Mr. Grant?"

"Sophia and I met her at her sister's wedding."

"Her sister is married? That is a welcome development. Odd that I did not see the banns."

"Um, well, she…that is to say…she eloped."

"I see." There was a pause. The earl's voice grew softer. "That must have been hard for her father."

"Apparently, he did not approve for some reason."

"There may have been no reason."

Tobias cocked his head to the side. "That doesn't make sense, Uncle."

"Nevertheless, it is likely true. And you say you attended this wedding?"

"With Sophia, yes."

"And you met Miss Sangford there? Is she a friend of the family? As I understand it, Miss Grant specifically invited her to the poetry reading."

"No." Tobias gritted his teeth. The memory of that she-devil was still very fresh in his mind. She had come so close to tearing him and Sophia apart. A vicious, unfeeling woman who would have as pleasantly destroyed anything in her path as sipped a cup of tea. "No," Tobias repeated. "She is a friend to no one. Certainly not friendship of the kind you or I would undertake."

"And yet she was at the wedding?"

"She was at the church with a fr… a person as ill-suited to friendship as herself. They had an appointment with the vicar.

And she recognized Sophia's sister. She quickly deduced the rest."

"And this is the secret you have kept from me? The fact that you attended these clandestine nuptials?"

Tobias rubbed the back of his hand. This wasn't getting any easier.

"Unfortunately, this is only where the matter began."

His uncle sat back in his chair. "Go on."

"When Miss Sangford realized who I was, she blackmailed me."

"And who are you to be blackmailed?" the earl asked with a tilt to his head.

"Sophia's secret beau, and your nephew."

"Ah." His uncle nodded, seeming to understand. "She wanted money for her silence on your relationship."

"I'm afraid it's worse than that."

"Tell me."

"She wanted an introduction to you."

"To *me*? Why?"

By now, Tobias was in a sweat. His uncle, by comparison, was entirely calm, the truth of his betrayal still eluding him. But that was about to change.

"She... Well, the fact is...she hoped to... I mean... She thought she could capture your affection, and with it, your wealth and title." The miserable words were finally said. Tobias bowed his head in shame.

Of all the things his uncle might say, of all the reactions Tobias had imagined, what followed so shocked him that he could only stare, aghast.

Uncle Edmund laughed. He laughed loud and long. Tears of mirth gathered and were dabbed away with a long finger, while he continued to chortle. Tobias could only watch, mystified, until his uncle finally reached for his handkerchief and noisily blew his nose. He folded and returned it to his pocket, patting the dark fabric and then wiping his eyes with the heel of his palm once more.

"Poor Miss Sangford," he said, slightly more serious now. "What a disappointment for her. Though from what Lord Howell told me, not entirely undeserved."

"What did he say?" Tobias asked, still dazed from the turn of events.

"Just that he'd seen her entering the library after me and rushed to warn me of her—shall we say—interests. It had taken longer than he'd liked because he'd had to wade through a tide of enthusiastic mothers trying to introduce their daughters. But that is neither here nor there. The point is, she had tried her luck with him before."

"The nerve of that woman," Tobias said more in wonderment than anger. "What does she think qualifies her for such a match?"

"Of course, she never stood a chance," his uncle agreed. "The viscount is an excellent judge of character, especially for one so young."

"No wonder she was so facetious toward him in the library."

"Miss Sangford's reaction to being rejected was unpleasant, to say the least." His uncle shook his head. "Sour grapes, you know. She spoke rather uncharitably about the viscount, which only made it harder for him to find a suitable match. Rather like your Miss Dunbar."

"I wish you wouldn't call her that," Tobias said sulkily.

Uncle Edmund waved a perfunctory hand. "You know what I mean." He placed his palms firmly on the desk. "Right, shall we get back to it?"

"Sorry?"

"I assume we're done. You met a woman of low substance who threatened to tell your secret unless you introduced her to me. You did so. As you can tell"—he shrugged—"we are not now, in fact, courting. Your secret connection with Miss Grant is safe, albeit unresolved. Was there anything else?"

"I went behind your back," Tobias explained, feeling a little foolish for having to clarify to his uncle what, exactly, his wrongdoing had been. "I arranged a scenario that put you at risk, protecting Sophia and myself instead of you. But Miss Sangford said that she would only guarantee her silence if I remained silent too."

"A difficult situation, and most unfortunate. I am glad it is resolved."

"Uncle." Tobias threw up his palms in exasperation. "Why aren't you angry with me?"

"Do you want me to be?"

"Yes! Well…obviously not. But I do not know how to ask your forgiveness if you don't feel wronged."

His uncle folded his hands. "Did you believe I was truly at risk from this dubious woman?"

"I hoped not. But I could not be sure."

"And if she had succeeded?"

"I would have said something then."

"Even if she had carried out her threat?"

"Yes."

"Then I was never truly at risk."

Tobias processed this.

"I wish to apologize, anyway," he said. "It is not the way I mean to conduct myself. I have nothing but the utmost respect for you, Uncle. I would hate for you to lose your trust in me."

The worry must have shown upon his face, for his uncle paused to contemplate it. The seconds ticked by, each an eternity of guilt, regret, and hope. The relief when the earl finally spoke was so profound, Tobias was willing to accept whatever harsh words his uncle might have for him, just to be done with them.

"Tobias." The tone was firm, but kind. "You are not a deceitful chap by nature. I have seen you struggle with that aspect of your relationship with Miss Grant. You have only accepted its necessity for her sake. It was likely the same when dealing with Miss Sangford. And yet, there is a line you will not cross. That, my boy, is an important difference, and I recognize it."

The love and understanding from this man whom Tobias so

valued hit him squarely in the chest with the *thunk* of an arrow. It was a blow of mercy, and yet it hurt. He didn't deserve it. But, oh, how he cherished it!

"Now," his uncle continued, "do I approve of subterfuge in general? Certainly not. But I am not so rigid in my thinking that I cannot allow for the complexities of human nature. In short, you may rest easy. All is well between us."

Tobias felt a lump form in his throat. He could not speak. He had no words. He nodded vigorously, then looked away, as even this small act brought more emotion to the surface.

Uncle Edmund waited patiently and without embarrassment as Tobias pulled himself together. It took a little longer than Tobias cared to admit. Weeks of anxious fretting were not so easily smoothed away. He was immensely grateful for his uncle's calm reason. It was a big part of why he had not thought Miss Sangford a real danger to him.

As his emotions settled, a thought he had tucked away, almost unnoticed, in the back of his mind now rose up and demanded attention. It was really none of his business. He should probably just leave it alone. After all, his uncle had been so accommodating, he had no right to…

"Uncle," he said, before his good sense could talk him out of it, "why did Miss Sangford never stand a chance? Her charm was so convincing, it was chilling to watch. And yet you gave her no thought other than what civility demanded. And what did Mr. Grant mean when he said you understood about sorrow, and something that happened long ago? I don't wish to pry. It just puzzles me."

"It is personal," his uncle said.

"Oh." Tobias could not hide his disappointment.

"But no secret."

Curiosity flickered back to life. "If it is uncomfortable to talk about…" Tobias ventured.

Uncle Edmund exhaled deeply. "It is not uncomfortable in the sense of shame or embarrassment. But I do not enjoy reliving the past. It lives with me regardless. And that is enough."

Tobias sat on tenterhooks. Would it end there? Would his uncle say more? He waited in breathless silence. And then…

"I had thought your mother may have told you, but I suppose she did not think it necessary. You were just a very small boy."

Tobias did not respond, afraid to discourage his uncle with a misplaced phrase.

"I had a wife. I had a child." He swallowed. "Children."

The news hit Tobias like a stone. And above the shock, floated the terrible word. *Had.*

"Did she…? Did they…?" Tobias could not bring himself to utter his fears aloud.

"Yes. It was a difficult birth. There were twins. The boy came first. My son. My heir."

His uncle winced.

"The midwife thrust him into my arms. I did not notice her urgency. I only noticed the way his fingers curled over the blanket he was swaddled in. I tucked my finger inside his tiny hand, marveling at his miniature perfection. Grateful for the life that had been added to ours."

Dread seeped into Tobias's heart, knowing what must follow.

"I stood in the hallway, my son safely in my arms, when the door the midwife had rushed to close slowly creaked open and revealed all."

Tobias no longer wished to hear more. But it was too late. He must share his uncle's sorrow now, the price of his curiosity.

"My wife was bleeding. I have never seen so much blood…" His uncle's voice cracked. His narration ceased.

Tobias felt his world tilt. All this time, his uncle had carried this image of his wife. This terrible scene had branded his heart with pain and loss. Tobias could scarcely believe that he had the will to tell more. But he did—with a strength that Tobias could not conjure the equal of. Perhaps he needed to tell all, to shift from that moment of horror to the outcome, to release it once again to the ether of the universe. But if Tobias thought what would follow would be easier, he was wrong.

"She was too weak to push our daughter out," his uncle said, his voice rough and low. "The midwife looked to me, and I deduced her meaning clearly. There was nothing more she could do. We could not save my wife. But we could save the baby. We must send for the doctor at once."

"I sat with my wife. My son and I together. I placed him in her arms. She was barely conscious. But she tilted her head against his. With the last of her breath, she kissed his tender cheek. By the time the doctor came, she was gone. Our daughter was stillborn. Within a week, our son joined them. He had come too soon. He needed his mother. He went to be with her."

"I am so sorry," Tobias said, though his words fell short of the terrible emotion they expressed. "I understand now." Yet how little he understood! It was a scene of tragedy beheld from afar. Empathy and compassion arose from the sight, but he could never truly understand the magnitude of such an experience from this great a distance. In a way, he as grateful it was so. To share a full understanding, he would have to share fully in the suffering. With Sophia so very much still with him, he did not *want* to know more. The thought of losing her in the same way... No, it did not bear thinking about.

What he did understand now was his uncle's solitude. How could another woman ever hold his attention? He had nothing left to give. All he had ever loved had been wrenched from him. Who could compare to the perfection with which one regards a beloved in memory? And when one has suffered such immense loss, who would risk more?

"Do you have satisfaction?" His uncle's words jerked Tobias from his thoughts.

"Satisfaction, Uncle?" Tobias stared at the man before him. How could satisfaction result from such a revelation?

"You had questions, about my conversation with Mr. Grant, and about my immunity to the charms of women. Do you have the answers you sought?"

Tobias lowered his head. "I am ashamed to have asked. I had not meant to make you relive such a brutal experience."

"You did nothing more than my own memory demands of me every day. That is why I fill my mind with books and art—to squeeze out any room for these thoughts to creep in. Your curiosity only meant I spoke them aloud. But they are with me always."

"Then," Tobias said after some thought, "the best remedy I can offer is to let us resume our work."

Uncle Edmund surfaced a little from his gloom. "Yes," he answered, "that's the very thing. A good book. Preferably one with complex notions, so that I may immerse myself entirely in deciphering them." His gaze fell longingly on the volumes Tobias had brought. "But first, I think, a letter to my agent." He cast about him for paper to write on.

Tobias handed him a blank sheet and a feeble smile of support. He had not yet learned what his uncle had mastered—to throw layers of calm over his tangled feelings. He prayed he would never have to.

"Thank you, my boy," his uncle said, reaching across the desk. As he took the page, he paused, his eyes firmly upon Tobias. "You know, I often think my son would have been a lot like you. At least, it would have pleased me if he were."

"Th-Thank you, Uncle," Tobias stuttered. "That is to say… I mean… You are…" He lapsed into helpless quiet.

"And Miss Grant is every bit the daughter I wish I had known. In fact, I think I shall write to a few of my contacts and see what can be done with her current work-in-progress. I know you have both devoted much of your time and skill to it. If it is anything like the excellent material I heard at the reading, there should be no difficulty at all acquiring a publisher for her second anthology."

Tobias opened his mouth, only to be silenced before he even had a chance to speak.

"No," his uncle protested, "you may not run off and write to

Miss Grant about it. Let's not get ahead of ourselves. I shall make the necessary inquiries. And when you next see her, perhaps she could provide some samples of what they might expect if they are interested. Mind you, I make no promises."

A thousand different responses rushed Tobias's brain all at once, congesting the natural flow to his tongue so that, instead of his usual deluge of speech, Tobias could only offer wordless wonder. It was the third time in as many minutes that he had been robbed of speech, and he took it as a sign to attempt it no further. He merely nodded and restricted his answer to a heartfelt "Thank you."

For his uncle, it seemed enough. He immediately set to work on his letters, peace descending once more as his tortured mind was relieved of its heaviest burden, if only for a while.

For Tobias, his thoughts turned, as always, to Sophia. How animated those bright eyes of hers would become when she heard the news! She would throw her arms around him and reward him simply for being the messenger. A flush of concentration would touch her cheeks as she pondered which poems to send. She would argue none were good enough. He would watch her fret, agitated and earnest in always giving her best. He would kiss her fingertips and tell her that she was most beautiful when she fussed. And she would glare at him, only to catch the hint of passion that lay shallow in his breast, and lose her train of thought.

After all the challenges, troubles, and difficult conversations of the past several weeks, he could not wait for Monday to come. A day with Sophia. A day closer to one day calling her his wife.

CHAPTER TWENTY

TOBIAS WAS WATCHING Sophia read, her head bent in concentration. She tucked an errant curl behind her ear. A single gray strand threaded through the twist of dark hair. He knew she was self-conscious about her age and the subtle signs that gave it away. As far as he was concerned, it added character to her beauty. Just like the smear of ink on her elegant hand. Once it had even stained her chin. He grinned. She would be mortified when she discovered it. But he was enjoying the imperfection of her loveliness.

"What about this word here?" Sophia pointed.

Tobias did not look.

"I will not offer my opinion," he said. "I have told you there is nothing more to be done. Your work is ready. I will take it with me today and have my uncle read it. He will know which publisher would want the honor of printing it."

"I don't know. You are hardly an unbiased judge."

"Why? Because I love you? Or because I knew your work was excellent before we spent weeks polishing it?"

"Both," she said, squirming a little.

Seeing her discomfort under the weight of his bold affection was nothing new to Tobias. She would just have to grow used to it.

"In that case, I defer you to my uncle. He will offer you an honest perspective."

"Yes, I know. That is why I only want to present my very best to him."

"And this manuscript," Tobias declared as he began gathering up the pages, "is precisely that."

Sophia's grip tightened on the sheet she held.

"You may keep it if you wish." Tobias shrugged. "I know all your poems by heart by now. I will simply rewrite that one and add it to the rest."

Sophia released the page with a scowl.

"You always win," she muttered sulkily.

"And you're the only one who *wants* to."

Tobias leaned closer and kissed her on the tip of her nose. She folded her arms.

He tilted his head and touched his lips to her cheek. No response.

His mouth opened slightly and slid down to hers. Her lips resisted for but a moment, then parted and pressed against the warmth of his. Her arms loosed and slipped around his shoulders, scooping his neck toward her. The silk of her dress rustled as she shifted her weight against him, the fullness of her breasts pushing against his ribs.

Tobias groaned as pleasure washed over him. He fought to think clearly. How he wanted her! But not like this. Not under her father's roof.

He pulled back, drawing his fingers along the silky skin of her arms. He folded his hands around hers and brought them to his lips.

"You are not playing fair," he murmured.

She flashed him a coy smile. "I don't know what you mean."

"Yes, you do. Stop being irresistible. How am I supposed to keep my distance?"

"Who said I wanted you to?" Her voice grew husky and her lips gathered in a pout.

"Marry me, then, Sophia."

At once, the shutters came down.

Her gaze dropped away. She tucked her hands into her lap. Her posture grew stiff, and her voice filled with starch.

"I'm not ready."

"Don't you want the same happiness as your sister?"

"I am not my sister."

"Look, I know she followed a more daring path. But I will not ask that of you. Let me make my formal application to your father. I know I am not a wealthy man, but my connection to the Earl of Carthige must count for something. If we choose to remain at my uncle's estate, you will even be near your family. I cannot imagine what protest your father might have. I do think it is time, my darling."

Sophia remained unmoving. "For that which you ask, there will never be a time that is right."

"How can that be? What could your father have against me?" Tobias halted abruptly as a worrying truth bubbled up. "We will not tell him of our secret meetings, surely? It was not how I wanted things. You know that. We must begin again. Do it right this time. Once he comes to know me, he will have no doubt that we are well-suited."

"I fear that is exactly where the trouble will start."

Tobias cocked his head to the side. "You have quite lost me."

Sophia sighed. "Papa will never give me permission to marry you, Tobias."

"Well," Tobias said cautiously, "strictly speaking, we don't need his permission. We are both of age."

"But he won't give his blessing."

"Never? Not even if we are patient and show him how happy we can make each other?"

"*Especially* not then."

"That doesn't sound very reasonable."

"No."

Tobias pondered this a minute. "Do we...?" He hesitated. "Do we *need* the blessing of an unreasonable man?"

Sophia turned her eyes upon him. Pain filled them, fathoms deep. "If I marry, he will cut me off completely. No inheritance. No contact. Not with anyone still in this house. Not ever again."

A shocked silence rippled out across the room.

Eventually, Tobias managed to splutter, "But...but...but *why?*"

Sophia rubbed her fingertips against her temple, then cupped her hand around the back of her neck, massaging the tension in it. She closed her eyes and sighed deeply. "Because he mourns," she said simply. "He mourns my mother still. He is lost without her. She brought balance to his life. Now he is like a man whose foot is nailed to the floor. He goes around and around in circles and makes no progress. Mother was the only one who could have talked sense into him. And we are all that is left of her. To lose any of us is to lose her all over again."

Tobias sucked in his breath. "I see. Well, I can certainly sympathize with his sorrow." His thoughts turned to his uncle. Their conversation was still raw in his mind. His loss had been so complete. At least Mr. Grant had a house full of children as comfort. Children who could marry and give him grandchildren. Why would he not welcome that? "It seems to me," Tobias said with some confusion, "that marriage *adds* to his family rather than takes something from him."

"He does not see it that way."

"I'm afraid my compassion for him must be rather limited if these are his terms."

Sophia shook her head. "There is no logic to it. His agony has necessarily become ours. Misery has corrupted our father's heart. Already, it is forbidden to mention Adriana at all. It is as if she never existed. He has cut her out like a festering wound. But it is a wound of his own making." Her fingers twisted into the black silk fabric of her skirt. "And we are all forced to share in his madness."

"Then let me free you from it!" Tobias urged. "Perhaps your sister was wise, after all. She has escaped to a better life. You can do the same."

"I am *not* my sister."

"What if all five of you stood up to him together? Surely, he will not want to lose you all? He *must* relent in the face of such a terrible prospect!"

"And if he does not? If all of us are left homeless and penniless and fatherless? What will become of Bess? She will have no prospects. And Henry will be forced to leave Cambridge."

"So, you would rather remain in this house where the shadow of death infects everything."

"You think I want this?" Sophia's eyes flashed with anger. "You think I enjoy having to choose between keeping my family and making one of my own?"

"No, of course not! I…"

"You think it is so simple. I should cast off my entire family for your sake. How is the price you are asking me to pay any lower than what my father exacts from me?" Her mouth twisted bitterly. "Sacrifice. Always sacrifice. My mother. My health. My freedom of choice."

Silence sank like lead between them.

"Sophia…"

"What? What is it? What lesson do you want me to learn this time? What must I change to live up to your expectations?"

"Nothing. Nothing at all. It has been a shock. That is all. I had no idea. How could I have known? You kept it from me."

"What choice did I have? Would you speak such secrets aloud?"

"I'm not blaming you. I am only asking for a little time to process what I have learned."

Sophia covered her face with her hands. "I am sorry." She moaned. "I should not take out my frustration on you. You have been true and constant." She lifted her head. Red-rimmed eyes strained to keep back tears. "It is to no avail, Tobias. You understand now. It was but a dream. And we have woken up."

"What are you saying?"

Sophia gave no answer.

Tobias leaned back in his chair, his hands on his knees. "I think you know me well enough, Sophia, to realize that this is not the end of it. Not by far. Happiness such as ours is rare indeed. I will not give it up. But I need to think on it further. And you need to rest. I will return next Monday, and we will speak more on this. You are right that I have woken up. My eyes are wide open. And I will seek a solution."

A pale hope lit Sophia's face, only to have it clouded over by the habit of helplessness. "There is no outcome that does not cause suffering," she answered.

"We are suffering already. We can only move forward. Which way is best, I cannot yet say. But I am determined to discover it."

He stood and reached over, planting a tender kiss upon her forehead. For a moment, the room was still, the mood one of fragile optimism.

For a moment.

Then, without warning, the door banged open, and Katie barged into the room. She all but shouted, "The master is on the drive!"

Sophia gasped, her face blanching with dread. "Get out, get out! Go, Tobias. Go now. Quickly!"

Tobias stood rooted to the spot. Indecision gripped him. Should he confront Mr. Grant? Was this a sign? But one look at the terror in Sophia's eyes and his mind was made up.

Sophia was groaning and rocking her head between her hands. "Why is he back so soon? What will he say? What will he *do?*"

Tobias snatched up the loose pages of the manuscript and quickly folded them as he made for the door. The sound of his boots crossing the floor was matched with footfalls approaching the room from without. Tobias froze.

Mr. Grant, his long hair wild from riding, strode into the room and halted in surprise. "Mr. Mannerly. What are you doing here?"

"I…uh…" Tobias floundered. He looked down for inspiration and spied Sophia's pages gripped in his hand. "Ah! Yes! I have come with good news for Miss Grant."

Mr. Grant's eyebrows rose. "Indeed? And what, pray tell, is the nature of this news that it could not have been shared in a letter?"

"Oh." Tobias hesitated. "Well…I confess I wished to deliver the news myself for the satisfaction of seeing the joy it might bring. As you know, I am an ardent admirer of Miss Grant." He hurriedly cleared his throat. "Of her work, I mean."

Straightening to his full height, Mr. Grant tightened his jaw and demanded stiffly, "I think you should explain yourself, sir."

"Gladly," Tobias answered. As you know, my uncle and I attended the excellent poetry reading last week. Finest event of its kind, if you ask me." He beamed at Sophia.

Her father nodded impatiently. "Yes, thank you. What has this to do with your news?"

"Well, due to his fervent love of books, Lord Carthige has many contacts in the world of literature. And he believes he knows several publishers who would be very interested in Miss Grant's next collection of works."

"She already has a publisher."

"But, Papa," Sophia interjected, "you had to invest a tidy sum to win his interest. This would be someone who recognizes the merit of my poems for their own sake."

"I see," Mr. Grant said, a little sulkily. "Then our publisher is no longer good enough. A little ironic, actually. I just came from a meeting with him. He wanted to say they are ordering a third print because the books we requested at the beginning of the month have already sold out. I did not want to wait until this evening to tell you." His lips tightened. "However, it is something of an anticlimax now, in light of Lord Carthige's news."

"Far from it!" Tobias cried. "It only speaks of the wisdom in your choice of publisher, sir, that they should invest further in their most talented client. More people should have the privilege of reading your daughter's exquisite writing." He gazed proudly at Sophia.

Mr. Grant looked at Tobias as if seeing him properly for the first time. His eyes narrowed.

"Thank you, Papa," Sophia said hastily. "You have brought me such encouragement. Not only now, but when you invested in the first print. My success really began with you."

Her father shifted his gaze to her.

"Nonsense, my dear. I simply did what any proud father would do—shamelessly boast to the world of his children's gifts."

"I must thank you, too, sir." Tobias beamed. "Without you, I would never have known Miss Grant existed."

"That is most kind," Mr. Grant answered. But his eyes darted from Tobias to Sophia, and the mechanisms of his brain did not appear to produce pleasing conclusions. "Shall I see you out, Mr. Mannerly? You have done what you came to do. Please thank your uncle for thinking of us." He looked at Sophia again. She sat primly, her eyes lowered, her mouth soft and undefiant. She was the very picture of an obedient daughter.

Tobias pitied her. How easily she slid into the role that was expected of her. It all made sense now. She was so willing to give up her own desires to appease others.

But enough was enough. She must shine in her own right. Not just as a poet, but as a person. He must see to it, no matter what.

He allowed her father to escort him out with only a polite bow to his dear Sophia. While Tobias waited for his horse to be brought to him, Mr. Grant stood like a sentry at the door. As soon as he had mounted up, the man took hold of the rein nearest him and looked Tobias dead in the eye.

"Mr. Mannerly, I thank you for your enthusiastic support of my daughter's writing. However, to arrive without warning, no matter your desire to personally see the results of your news, is unacceptable. Your uncle has no doubt informed you that we are a very private family. We have our reasons. It means we seldom receive visitors, and then by written invitation only. You are a gentleman and will respect this."

Tobias, despite his affable nature, was not one to be bullied. He returned the steady gaze and answered. "I am a reasonable man. All reasonable demands will be honored."

Mr. Grant blinked. Then he stood back. "I believe we understand each other. Good day to you, sir."

Tobias touched the tip of his hat, more out of habit than respect. He clicked his tongue and spurred his horse forward. As he rode down the drive, he could feel Mr. Grant's glare burning into the back of his neck.

His skin crawled. Fifteen years under that tyrant's thumb! It was a wonder Sophia had kept her bearings at all! Now, more than ever, he was determined to set her free from her gilded cage.

He must talk to his uncle. He needed the advice of a sensible person. If the earl didn't hold Tobias back, he was bound to do something foolish. He set his horse into a canter, then a gallop. His heart thudded along with the hoofbeats.

When he reached the stables, he threw himself out of the saddle, leaving the reins trailing and the stableboy scurrying to grab them. Tobias marched into the earl's study without knocking, causing the man to look up in surprise.

"Uncle, we must talk. Matters are worse than we thought."

Lord Carthige cast a longing look at the pages before him, then sighed and removed his glasses. He leaned back in his chair and braced himself. "Very well, Tobias. I do not know how I have come to take on the role of advisor to young lovers. It is certainly an unenviable task. But I will help where I can. Tell me everything."

CHAPTER TWENTY-ONE

SOPHIA TWIRLED A second time, and Katie clapped her hands in delight.

"Oh, miss, you look wonderful! The color suits you."

"I didn't realize how much I had missed it. You don't think it's too much?'

"It's only lilac, miss. Half-mourning. Most ladies are wearing it after a year. Some even six months. Come to think of it, I've never seen you in anything but black."

"Well, you've only been working for us for five or six years. So you wouldn't have."

"High time, then, if you don't mind my saying so, Miss Grant. And I know a certain gentleman who is sure to agree."

Sophia's hand traced the trim of lace at the low neckline. "Yes, Tobias will notice at once." Her hand whipped away and her wistful smile disappeared. "But so will Papa." She sat down quite suddenly, her legs tired from the brief exertion. "There will be questions. No doubt he will even draw conclusions. Accurate ones. But I must begin to stand up for the little things. If I cannot be bold in my small choices, I will never gain the courage to fight for the harder ones."

"You don't think he will be angry, miss? Not about something as harmless as this?'

"Oh, he won't see it as harmless. This is a much bigger step than perhaps you realize, Katie. I am signifying that I am coming out of mourning. I am the only one of his children who has lingered in it as long as he has. He will feel betrayed. Abandoned. He will feel I no longer honor the memory of my mother. And—more importantly—he will ask himself why. Why, all of a sudden, do I do this? He will make the connection with Mr. Mannerly's visit. And he *should*. I do not want to live in shadows anymore."

She spread her fingers across the soft-hued cotton. "I am not as bold as Adriana. I cannot shout and stamp my foot. Besides, that has never been the way to convince Papa of anything. Mama was always gentle in her manipulations. And he welcomed them, accepted them with love, just as they were done with love. If I am ever to resurrect his older, better self, that can be the only way. I must try. Tobias has been so patient, so willing to seek answers. I must match him in effort. Otherwise, I do not deserve him."

"Yes, miss," Katie replied. She added nothing more, though Sophia was certain she had much to say. "Shall I do your hair now?"

Sophia nodded, stood carefully, and walked the few steps to the chair that stood before her mirror. Katie began at once to fuss, and Sophia left her to her task.

On the vanity lay the letters Katie had smuggled upstairs. Adriana's pages were filled with joy. Sophia worried that her sister hid some sorrow beneath the effusion of happiness. But if she did, it was not obvious. Adriana had made her peace, it seemed. She was happy. Sophia did not begrudge her this. There had been enough unnecessary gloom in their home. What was the point of dwelling on things you could not change?

Tobias, as usual, wrote encouragements. His uncle had already passed her manuscript to a friend, confident that it would soon be in print. The thought of reaching this outcome without her father's help was incredibly freeing. It meant a possible independent income. Along with the small inheritance from her mother, she would have something to add to Tobias's allowance from his uncle. They could survive on this sum, if they had to.

She prayed it would not come to that.

Katie was taking forever. Sophia's hair had gradually become a complex pattern of loops and twists. With the final tuck and two more pins, Katie stood back and asked nervously, "What do you think?"

"It is…more complicated than I am used to," Sophia ventured. In truth, she did not like it. It did not feel like her. But Katie had been so keen.

"You don't like it."

"No, no, I…" Sophia stopped. What was it Tobias had said? She was always accommodating everyone else's feelings. Often at the cost of her own. She took a deep breath. "You have done the style very well, Katie. But I'm afraid it's just not *me*. I love the way you normally do it. I would prefer that."

Katie shrugged and began to unpin Sophia's locks. She brushed them out again, leaving them mostly loose and curling against her neck.

"You're right, miss. That does suit you better. The one before was too much."

"Thank you, Katie." Sophia took another deep, bolstering breath. "Now…for the real challenge. Let's see what Papa has to say about my dress."

Sophia sent for a footman to bring her to the drawing room. Katie followed with the writing tray.

Soon after, Mr. Grant popped his head in at the door.

"I see you are all settled for the morning," he remarked, taking in the scene. At once, his face dropped. "You are no longer in full mourning." The statement was simple. Yet it carried the weight of continents.

"No, Papa, I have grown tired of black." She kept her voice steady. "But I will always miss Mama in my heart, where it matters."

"I see." There was a long pause. Sophia could almost see the wheels turning in his mind. "What has brought about this sudden change?"

"It is not sudden. I have been considering easing my self-imposed restrictions for some weeks now. Today, I acted on it. Do you not like the color on me? I feel pretty. I have not felt pretty for such a long time."

The frown softened. Mr. Grant cleared his throat. "You look well. I am happy to see you thrive." He swallowed hard. "Your mother would have approved."

"Thank you," Sophia whispered shyly. "Your blessing means the world to me."

Mr. Grant was silent a while longer, though his thoughts were clearly not equally still. "I've been thinking…"

"Yes, Father?"

"Now that summer is approaching, perhaps it is time we planned a carriage ride together."

"I would like that very much."

"In fact, it is unusually warm today. Perhaps we might even risk a small excursion in the early afternoon."

"Oh! But it is Monday! You are always out on business on a Monday."

"Well, perhaps I have become too set in my ways. I have no pressing matters to attend to. I would like to treat you to an outing instead. I so often take the air with Bess. I am afraid I have rather neglected you."

Sophia's mind was in turmoil. What was her father's true motive? Did he want to keep an eye on her? Did he suspect Tobias would come again?

Her heart stopped. Tobias! She must warn him!

"I…er…had planned to catch up with my letters today," she stammered, her thoughts racing.

"Surely, they will not take the entire day to write?"

Oh, why did her father have to choose today to be persistent in his attention?

"I promised Lord Byron I would send him my comments on his latest poem. It would be poor form to make such a distinguished gentleman wait. And I must choose my words carefully so as not to misrepresent myself. You see my predicament."

"Very well. I, too, shall attend to my correspondence this morning. If you find yourself making good progress, we may yet fit in a ride while the air is warm. If not, we will both have spent the day productively."

"Er…yes. Of course. That is an excellent plan. Thank you for thinking of my needs, Papa."

"It is nothing. You know how important you are to me, Sophia."

"Yes, Papa."

"I shall join you for a light repast at lunch. Let us see how well we have applied ourselves by then."

"Certainly. I will begin at once."

Sophia could scarcely wait for her father to leave the room. She did not have a moment to lose.

"Katie, what shall I do? Tobias must be warned!"

"I could wait for him down the lane, miss, and stop him before he comes near the house."

"No, no, if Papa looks in on me while you are out, he will demand an explanation for your absence. I do not want to get you into trouble."

"What about the gardener? Thomas moves freely about the grounds. The master will not question where he is."

"But will he recognize Mr. Mannerly?"

"I think everyone knows your gentleman by now, miss. We sort of keep an eye out for him, if you'll pardon the cheek of it, miss."

"I don't know what to think of my affairs being spied on, but today, I am grateful for it. Here, let me write a quick note for you to take to Thomas. He is to give it to Mr. Mannerly, and no one else."

"Yes, miss."

Sophia scribbled a quick, untidy message. She folded and sealed it and sent Katie off in all haste, cautioning her to keep watch, lest the master see her.

She looked down at her dress. It had been a small triumph. And yet it seemed they made no progress. What was to become of their Mondays together? Did her father suspect Tobias's interest in her? Would he clamp down harder than ever on her freedom, never trusting her to be alone again? Or had he thought only of her and her fondness for a carriage ride? If he would truly consider what she wanted, she may yet win him over.

Katie returned promptly, assuring Sophia she had not been seen. If their plan worked, Tobias would return home, undetected by her father. Their secret would be safe.

It was small comfort. Their cherished time together today was lost. Once a week had been little enough. Now she couldn't be certain of any Monday.

The day stretched out interminably before her. It was impossible to concentrate on poetry. Instead, Sophia attempted some embroidery. It was only when Katie fetched her some tea an hour later—and brought news that Thomas had given Mr. Mannerly the note—that Sophia could at last breathe easier.

She settled a little and attempted to deal with her overdue correspondence, which proved a useful distraction. By the time her father had joined her for a light lunch, she had perked up a little and was ready to make the most of their outing together. After all, there was the chance that her father was simply in a good mood. Next week, all might be back to normal. Then again, was that the normal she wanted for herself?

Sophia wrestled with her thoughts until the footman announced that the carriage was ready. Once she was snuggly wrapped up within the compartment, her father seated himself opposite her, smiling benevolently. The coachman clicked his tongue and the horses shifted into motion. The reminder of her recent rides with Tobias brought a warm glow to her heart—and an ounce of courage. She knew what she wanted. She would not give him up. And if her father truly cared, he would not ask her to.

It was a big leap, too much for one conversation. She was not that brave, nor could she expect her father to change his thinking in an instant. But she could take a step in the right direction.

She licked her dry lips. "Papa."

"Yes?"

"There is something I wish to share with you."

"I am listening."

"I have learned something new about myself."

"Indeed?"

The carriage wheels bumped and rolled. And Sophia's secrets jostled each other, nudging forward to be heard first. Where to begin?

"Something happened while you were away two months ago, and it has changed the way I think about everything."

"Oh?" Papa cast his gaze to the window. "You would rather discuss this than enjoy the view?"

"It is more important."

"We so rarely take a ride together. Surely, it can wait."

"No. It can't."

"Hmm, perhaps I misunderstood your desire for time outdoors."

"That's not it. I…"

Realization hit her squarely between the eyes. He was afraid! Terrified, even. She knew, because all too recently, she had lived within fear's suffocating grip. She recognized its symptoms—the way he licked his dry lips, the fact that he could not look her in the eye, the numerous attempts at deflecting the conversation elsewhere. He was scared of what she would say. He did not want to hear her truth. He was not ready to confront that pain within himself.

Well, she was. She must push through the murky waters of her past toward the light, no matter how small each stroke. Tobias had shown her how to kick her way to the surface, instead of drowning in the past. The sweetness of her first breath of true freedom was within reach. And Sophia wanted to share its intoxicating reward with those she loved.

It was time to teach her father how to swim.

CHAPTER TWENTY-TWO

TOBIAS WAS PACING again. Lord Carthige had quite given up on his reading. He sat, fingers steepled, waiting for his nephew to subside a little.

"How will I see her again?" Tobias demanded of the universe in general and his uncle in particular. "If Mr. Grant has discarded a predictable schedule, Sophia and I cannot meet. How am I supposed to convince her to marry me if I cannot speak to her face to face?"

"I did warn you it would not be easy," his uncle reminded him.

"You did not say why!"

"I was unfamiliar with the full extent of the situation. I knew the death of his wife cast a lasting shadow over that house. I knew they kept largely to themselves. But I had no idea the extreme consequences Grant would enforce should his children choose to marry. I would not have encouraged you to pursue the matter if I had known."

"But I *did* pursue it. And my heart is fully invested in Miss Grant. I cannot give up now. She has overcome so many challenges. What sort of man would I be if I just left her to fend for herself? She needs to know I will stand by her, no matter what."

"And will you?"

"Yes! I just don't know how."

"You will have to make up your mind sooner rather than later, I'm afraid."

Tobias swiveled to face his uncle. "What do you mean?"

"Come autumn, I will be traveling to Italy."

"Italy? That is very sudden."

"Not at all. I have been giving it some thought for a while now. We would have spoken of it sooner. But you have been…distracted."

"How long will you be away?"

"At least six months. I had intended for you to join me. I will be frequenting the museums and art galleries and studying ancient manuscripts. It is the sort of experience you would be well suited to." Uncle Edmund chewed his lip ponderously. "I had thought, if Miss Grant were to become Mrs. Mannerly, she would benefit from visiting there also. The winters in southern Italy are milder than ours, which would be kind to her health. And she would no doubt cross paths with some of the great literary artists who are drawn there as we are."

"It is a very generous offer, Uncle. I wish I could be sure Sophia would come. As things stand, though, I can be sure of nothing."

"I think you should make preparations to join me, regardless of the outcome with Miss Grant."

"That is a cold summons, sir. You know I cannot just abandon Sophia."

"I am sorry to say, you may not have a choice. If she rejects the idea of marriage, it would be wise to have something else to occupy your mind. Better to mend a broken heart in Italy than here, where you are constantly reminded of her."

"There is no place in all the world where I could escape my feelings for her."

Lord Carthige looked pointedly at him. "Yes, I imagine that is probably true."

"Besides," Tobias reminded him, "there is still the possibility of things ending well for us. I cannot see the path before me clearly, but I am determined to discover it."

"All the more reason to plan for Italy. If Miss Grant chooses to elope, she will need that distance from her father. Allow the dust to settle, so to speak. I would not normally speak so flippantly of such a serious infraction against societal norms, but I see how these circumstances warrant the consideration of less-than-ideal solutions."

Tobias did not like either scenario. There was pain, no matter what. All he wanted was to hold his darling Sophia and never have to leave her again. The price for love should not be this high. Why could they not be like other couples who met, fell in love, married—a thrilling spectacle enjoyed by all who observed? Why should her father withhold his blessing?

Tobias straightened suddenly.

Why, indeed?

"Uncle, would you excuse me awhile? I have a…"

"Letter to write? Of course you do. You are aware, I suppose, that the library will never be fully catalogued in my lifetime if I am the only one working at it?"

Tobias had the good grace to look ashamed.

"You have been more than patient with me. If you are willing to humor me a little longer, I will not only return to my task but may soon have the assistance of my wife to help us in our endeavor."

"There is no need to sweeten the pot, Tobias. Just write to Miss Grant and let us get back to the work at hand."

"Oh, it is not Miss Grant I am writing to. No, there is some-one else who owes me a written invitation."

Uncle Edmund raised an eyebrow. He shook his head and rolled his eyes heavenward. "I am reminded once again that I am not a young man. In many ways, I never have been. You have more energy and optimism than I have ever laid claim to, Nephew. I can only hope they serve you well."

"They have not failed me yet," Tobias called over his shoulder with a grin. Then he fairly skipped from the room.

Mr. Grant loved his children. Of that Tobias was certain. He just needed to remind the man of what love was supposed to *do*.

CHAPTER TWENTY-THREE

I F HER FATHER could have called her into his study to stand, submissive, on the rug before him, Sophia was certain he would have done so. Instead, he loomed over her where she sat on the chaise lounge, Katie having been sent from the room.

"What have you to do with this?" he demanded, thrusting a paper toward her.

Sophia took the page, recognizing Tobias's handwriting even from a distance.

Her father gave her no chance to read it before grumbling, "It's unheard of. The audacity. He must have been encouraged." He glared at her. "Well?"

"Give me but a moment, Father," Sophia answered, rapidly skimming over the letter. And then, "Oh. I see."

"Quite."

"It is not, in fact, unusual for a neighbor to request a visit."

"All our neighbors know better."

"He is new to the area."

"His uncle should have warned him."

"He likely did not think to ask his uncle's permission to act civilly."

Papa must have picked up on her sardonic tone, for he gave her a quizzical look before folding his hands behind his back. "You seem to support his wish to see me."

"It does not seem unreasonable."

"I intend to say *no*."

Sophia stiffened. "For what reason?"

"For the same reason I do not receive other visitors—I do not wish to. The sooner they understand that, the sooner we may resume normality."

"Normality?" Sophia was tired. Tired of living like this. Tired of denying herself. Tired of carrying her father's sadness. It was enough. If she did not speak up now, she was accepting that her father's world would forever be hers. And it was *not* normal. "It is an odd choice of words for the way we live," she declared.

Her father narrowed his eyes. "I do not like your tone, daughter. I would expect that from Adriana, but not from you."

"Oh," Sophia responded, the bitterness shallow in her words, "are we using her name again?"

She could see confusion flit across her father's face—a rapid blink of his eyes, a momentary frown, then a blank expression.

"What has come over you?" he finally managed to say.

"Nothing." *Everything*, she wanted to scream. *Everything has changed! I have found unconditional love, real acceptance, true purpose. And you would have me give it all up. To be a shadow of all I should be.* But she bit her tongue. She must be calm. *Softly does it.* He must hear the truth, but it must not frighten him. It must free him. If he could release the grip of his sorrow, they would all be free.

"Nothing?" he said with obvious disbelief. "I think not. Yesterday, you told me that you wish to marry one day, spoiling a perfectly good carriage ride. And today, you are petulant. This is not my Sophia."

Sophia folded her hands resolutely upon her lap. "If you think back far enough, Father, you will remember a Sophia exactly like this."

"She was a child."

"Who was never allowed to grow up."

"I beg your pardon?"

"Telling you that I can see myself getting married at some

point should not have ruined anything. It should not even have needed saying. All grown women think in this way. Their families encourage it. And Adriana was right to claim it for herself."

Sophia watched as her father ballooned with indignation. "What right have you to speak to me in this fashion? I am your father!"

Such a claim would previously have stopped Sophia in her tracks. Today, however, she remained resolute.

"Papa, do you remember a time when you were happy?"

"I will not suffer to be spoken to…"

"It was when Mama was alive. We were all happy then. And we all miss her. But she would be devastated to see what our family has become."

Her father's face grew flushed as he leaned toward her, an angry finger extended. "Sophia, you go too far…"

"No, Papa, it is *you* who have gone too far. And I have shared in your reckless sorrow because I felt I was to blame."

Her father pulled up short. "What do you mean? How were *you* to blame?"

"Because Mama became sick with my illness."

"I don't understand. How is that your fault?"

"It isn't. But all these years, I believed it was. And the more you mourned her loss, the heavier the blame sat upon my shoulders."

Her father became very quiet. "That is a heavy burden."

The silence in the room thickened.

"You carry the weight of it now?" he asked at last.

Sophia took a deep breath. "No, Papa, Tobias helped me."

"I'm sorry, who?"

"Mr. Mannerly. He… He makes me happy."

Her father's face puckered into a scowl. "You know him well enough to say such things?"

Sophia ignored his anger. It had already been allowed to reign for far too long. "It is possible to mourn Mama and still know love, as she did."

Her father's expression was pure thunder, his eyes dark, his lips wet with spittle. "You have no right to use your mother to justify your betrayal!"

She locked eyes with her father and said, in a voice that was both soft and pure iron, "I will speak of Mama. I will speak of Adriana. I will speak of Tobias. And I will love them, Papa, and you, for as long as I live. And you will make room in your heart for this. For your heart is too big to go without love. That is why you have filled it up with all this foolishness. Yes, foolishness, Papa. And you will let it go now. I, your daughter, ask it of you."

"I will… You can't… This isn't…" Papa's spluttering drew to a halt.

Sophia threw off the rug that warmed her legs, swinging them carefully to the floor.

"What are you doing?" Her father gasped.

She stood slowly and took a step forward. Then another. It was enough to cross the distance between them. She slipped her arms around him.

"Let it go, Papa. I am here."

"No," he cried, taking her wrists and peeling her free. "You wish to desert me, as your sister has!"

Sophia shook her head. "The only way to lose me is to force me to stay. You are throwing away the very things you wish to cling to. Just think, there could be grandchildren—beautiful little snuggly things with the same eyes or chin or cheeks as Mama's. We should lift up her memory to the light and celebrate it, not bury it deep in our hearts like a dark and lonely tomb."

Sophia's legs began to buckle. She stumbled backward toward the sofa. Her father lunged forward and gripped her wrists to steady her. He lowered her gently, then stepped back.

His eyes were upon her, but his mind was far away. The anger was gone. He looked quite lost, as if unsure what his rage should be replaced with. Sophia wished she could show him the way, but she had done all she could. The rest was up to him.

Her father stood, seemingly undecided, his expression giving

Sophia no clue as to whether she had reached him or not. He neither argued his cause nor accepted Sophia's. He merely stood, transfixed by thoughts Sophia could not decipher.

All at once, he turned on his heel and was gone. He disappeared so briskly that Sophia barely had enough time to call out "Papa!" to no avail. She sat, trapped by her impaired legs, unable to run after him, to comfort him, to insist he listen rather than draw back into his suffocating cocoon.

A part of her wished to send for a footman to be her legs. She imagined her father's chagrin at being chased down in this fashion and thought better of it. All she could do was allow him some time for her words to do their work, to seep into his heart and dissolve the barriers he had put up. Barriers that were meant to keep out more pain and loss, but, instead, had trapped these sensations within.

She had been brave, braver than she'd been in a full fifteen years. She had spoken up. She had stood her ground. Her father needed to process that the frightened, compliant Sophia was no more. He must remember how much he cherished that bold little girl who had once loved him with abandon and not trepidation. He must remember, and celebrate her return. She must give him time.

Time. It was in never-ending supply in this house, and yet she felt she did not have enough of it. Not the kind she wanted. Time with Tobias. Time with Adriana. Time filled with choice.

But she would claim it. Not much longer now. Her father would give his blessing, or she would go without. She had survived many hard years. She was strong enough. With Tobias at her side, she could conquer the world.

But it would all be much easier if she could only conquer her father first.

CHAPTER TWENTY-FOUR

FOR THE NEXT two days, Sophia's father avoided her. He did not come down for meals but ate in his room instead. He did not look in on her or plant a kiss upon her forehead or cheek. Nor did he ask after news from Lord Carthige's publisher. It was as if he had vanished entirely from her life.

Even George and Bess were neglected. Her brother bore it better than Bess. He could escape to a business appointment or ride into town. In fact, he might have felt his father's foot lifted somewhat from his neck. But Bess, like Sophia, was trapped within the house and its grounds. With the reigning mood so dark, it was all their youngest sibling could do not to cry with frustration.

Was this going to be their new normal? Had he given up entirely? Perhaps he no longer cared what any of his children did. Sophia could picture him, morose and depressed, skulking like a ghost in a corner of his own home.

Enough was enough.

At her insistence, a footman placed a chair outside the door of her father's study. She, in turn, was placed upon the chair. She waited until the footman had retreated before she knocked on the door.

"What is it? I gave instructions not to be disturbed."

"Papa, it is Sophia."

A lengthy silence followed. Then, a surly and quite unreasonable response.

"Go away."

Sophia's eyebrows pricked up.

"That is easier said than done," she remarked.

Another pause.

"If you found your way to my door, you can manage your way back."

"The footman has left. I am alone here. Would you like me to scream for help? Or shall I drag myself across the floor so that you may have peace?"

There was only a brief hesitation this time before the sound of footfalls signaled that her father was approaching the door. He pulled it open and glared at her.

"What do you want? I thought you would have eloped with Mr. Mannerly by now."

Sophia ignored him and peered inside the room.

"That settee looks far more comfortable than this chair. Would you mind?" She lifted her arms up to him to be carried.

He looked at Sophia, then at the settee, and finally, cast a glance down the corridor. For an awful moment, Sophia thought he was going to fetch a footman himself to take her away. Instead, he reached down wordlessly and collected her in his arms, grunting a little as he did so.

"You've grown heavier," he complained as he carried her across the room.

"I've grown up."

"Yes," he muttered, "that seems to be the problem in general."

"You would rather I hadn't?"

He put her down a bit more roughly than the strong, young footman would have done. Then he pushed his palms against his lowered back and grimaced.

"I'm getting old."

"So am I, Papa. But," she said cheerfully, "in some ways, I

have my whole life ahead of me."

Her father scowled at her comment. "Well, then, why aren't you off living it? And take Bess with you so that I don't have to endure my last daughter abandoning me when I least expect it."

"You really are impossible!" Sophia cried. "No one is abandoning you. Now stop being so petulant and come sit beside me."

When her father did not respond, she placed her hand on the seat next to her and added, "This is a welcome space. Why don't you make the most of it?"

He obeyed—though not with good grace—and sat, facing forward, his hands pressed upon his knees as if he were ready to spring up again at a moment's notice.

"I've let you in," he grumbled. "I've carried you. I've sat. What else do you command?"

"Don't be churlish, Papa," Sophia scolded. "Mama would never have stood for it."

"Your mother is gone."

"That," declared Sophia, "is not where the problem lies."

Her father turned toward her in surprise. "What do you mean?"

"The difficulty is that she is *not* gone. She is everywhere, in everything you see and do. And, most importantly, she lives on in us. You hear her voice when Adriana speaks. You see your reflection in Bess's eyes as if they were Mama's. George has her dignity, Henry her sense of humor. And I, her artistic flair, though I sketch the world through words. We keep the memory of her alive. When her image begins to fade from your mind, you reawaken it through us. We are her heartbeat, her warm breath. If we go, she goes. And you are terrified of losing her completely."

"Stop! That is enough!" Her father was shaking now, his skin clammy with distress.

But Sophia persevered. She must pull the barrier down with her bare hands if need be. She could no longer protect him. The only way to save her father was to hold him at the edge of the cliff and show him the danger before he pushed his entire family onto the rocks below.

"She was a wonderful woman, worthy of the degree to which you mourn her. But the manner in which you sustain it cannot continue. You cling so tightly to her memory that you have placed a strangling hold upon us all, squeezing the life out of us. And we have been so afraid to cause you further suffering that we have let you do it. We have not flourished. We have not dreamed of a life beyond these walls. We have claimed no other love for ourselves. And it has not helped you heal. Instead, we have morphed into a monstrous version of family, a miserable, haunted imbroglio. That is why Adriana left. That is why we will all choose to leave, or accept this fate as our final doom."

She touched her father's arm, a small act to reassure him that there was still hope and compassion, here, in this space, in this moment.

A strange guttural sound escaped his throat. Sophia jerked her hand back in alarm. His chest heaved. His shoulders scrunched forward. His arms folded in and he hugged himself. A rasping intake of breath followed, then a whimper, until finally her father's body became wracked with anguished sobbing.

"Oh, Papa!" Sophia reached for him again. "Papa, I am here. Give me your hand. Everything will be all right."

Her father looked up at her, at the extended hand. Through stuttered weeping, he unfolded his arms from his fetal pose. His hand took hers, gripping it as if it steadied him in a storm. Sophia held on to him until, gradually, his tears became a sniffle. He wiped his eyes roughly with his shirt sleeve.

"I am so ashamed," he finally said, his voice hoarse from crying. "You must hate me."

Sophia fixed an honest gaze upon her father. "I do not," she declared. "But it was hard to accept what you had let yourself become."

"How did I not see it?" He groaned. "All this time. The harm I have done..."

"It's not too late. We all love you. We have just been waiting for you to find your way back to us."

Her father smiled weakly. "You are so like your mother. She always knew how to guide me."

"Thank you, Papa."

He hung his head. "Adriana is like me. Willful. Stubborn."

"And yet she is my dearest friend."

The smile widened, then flickered and was gone. "I must make amends. So many years have been lost."

"But not all."

"No, not all." Her father pondered this, nodding to himself. Then he looked up at Sophia. "I don't know where to start."

How long Sophia had waited for this! How many times she had imagined the conversation, without ever finding the courage to go through with it. Now, here they were, on the other side of it, ready to move forward. She knew exactly what must come next. "A letter to Adriana," she announced. "Then, perhaps, a family meeting?"

"Yes, yes, I will begin at once." Her father cast an anxious glance at her. "How can I ever make it up to you? You have suffered most of all."

How strange, thought Sophia. Now that they had stepped back from the cliff once and for all, she felt no suffering. Nor would she dwell on what she had felt in the past. Rather, peace settled upon her like a healing mist. Within that peaceful center arose an image of Tobias, who had shown her the way. All that had stood between them was now dissolved, their paths converging at last, fully and completely. It just needed one final boulder to be rolled out of the way.

"Well..." Sophia's lip twitched into a coy smile. "If you really want to make it up to me, I believe there is a neighbor who deserves an invitation..."

CHAPTER TWENTY-FIVE

TOBIAS WAITED OUTSIDE the study of Mr. Grant like a schoolboy waiting to see the headmaster. His neckcloth felt too tight. His collar itched. His heart beat a mile a minute.

He had expected the man to keep him waiting—a power play of sorts. But he stood uncomfortably for less than a minute before the door swung open and Mr. Conrad Grant appeared.

"Do come in, Mr. Mannerly," he said, walking ahead to his desk and seating himself behind it. He indicated with an open palm, and Tobias strode forward to accept the chair facing his host and the sunny window.

"Thank you for receiving me, sir. I know it is a rare privilege."

Mr. Grant merely nodded. "Your uncle is well, I presume?"

"Yes, and he sends his best wishes," Tobias answered, suppressing the nerves that were starting to get the better of him.

"Well, here we are, then. How can I help you? I got the impression this was not to be purely a social call. That is partly why I entertained the idea of your visit. I am not a very sociable man, as I am sure you've heard."

Apprehension flooded Tobias's body, and his leg began to bounce in agitation. He pressed his hand firmly to his knee to stop it. "I appreciate your willingness to accommodate me," he replied, resisting the urge to squirm in his chair.

"Are you here on behalf of yourself or Lord Carthige? I am always willing to help a neighbor, whether they have been my frequent guests or not."

Tobias felt oddly tongue-tied. There was so much at stake. One wrong word and this chance would be lost. Best just to speak plainly, then. The truth was a straight path with fewer obstacles to trip over.

"I am here on behalf of myself…and Miss Grant."

"Oh?" Mr. Grant leaned back and cocked his head to the side. "That is a rather odd notion from a virtual stranger."

Heat crept up Tobias's neck and he imagined his flushed cheeks betrayed him.

"You should know, sir, that Miss Grant and I have been corresponding."

"I see. No doubt you discuss literature, as she does with several other gentlemen."

Tobias was taken aback by his host's calm response. "Er…yes, I am a great admirer of her poetry."

"As you should be. She is very talented."

"But…er…I am also an admirer of Miss Grant."

Mr. Grant's chin lifted. His eyes grew hooded. "What do you mean by that, sir?"

"You see, um…the more we wrote each other, the more I came to know the…er…woman…" Tobias swallowed hard. "The…er…woman behind the words, so to speak."

"You have feelings for my daughter?"

"Yes." Tobias breathed out his relief. There. It was finally out in the open. And the man had not yet thrown him out on his ear.

"And does she reciprocate these feelings?"

"That is my understanding, yes, sir."

"What do you plan to do about it?"

"Well, you see, I would like your permission to formally court your daughter, sir. To give you the opportunity to see I am an honorable man. And to reassure you that I do not intend to steal your daughter from you."

"Hmm. I assume you are referring to what happened with her sister."

"I cannot speak for another. I only know that I love Sophia. And she loves her family. I would never separate the two."

"Ah." Mr. Grant leaned back in his chair. "Then you do not wish to marry her."

"No! I mean, yes! I mean… I want very much to marry her. But I have no desire to injure her family in the process."

"So, in fact, you have not come to ask permission to woo her, but to request her hand in marriage."

"I suppose that is ultimately what I ask."

"Then you are asking the wrong person."

"Please, sir! Do not reject me out of hand. I only ask for a chance to prove myself. Sophia deserves as much. I know you have suffered great loss. I do not wish to add to your sorrow. Quite the opposite. I…"

"Have you quite finished?"

"No, sir! You must hear me on this. You misunderstand my intentions."

"I do not. I merely said you are asking the wrong person." Mr. Grant's face lit up with a broad smile.

But the smile was not for Tobias. It was focused on something behind him.

Tobias whipped round.

Sophia sat, beaming, in a chair against the back wall.

"Well?" said Mr. Grant. "Aren't you going to say something?"

Tobias was absolutely speechless.

"It seems, my dear," Sophia's father said, with what could only be described as mischief in his eyes, "your beau is quite mute on the subject. Perhaps we misunderstood his keenness to ask for your hand."

"You are a terrible tease, Papa," Sophia scolded. "Take pity on him."

"Do you see how she chastises me for your sake, Mr. Mannerly? I would say you are a very lucky man, indeed."

Tobias managed to summon a stunned, "Yes, sir" before staring in tongue-tied fascination at them both.

"Papa and I have spoken at great length, Tobias, but he would not allow me to forewarn you. He wanted to see what you were made of. I could not deny him that. We have kept so many secrets from him. He was entitled to one of his own."

Relief poured off Tobias in waves. Sophia and her father had spoken about his marriage proposal, and they were both smiling. How grateful he was to her father! And how proud he was of Sophia!

The next moment, he was across the room and kneeling before her. "You brilliant, beautiful creature!" he cried. "You have mended three hearts at once!"

Sophia cupped his face in her hands. "No, Tobias. It was you who made this possible. You, with your irrepressible spirit and constant devotion."

"Are the two of you going to argue about this all day?" Mr. Grant called across to them. "We've got a wedding to plan, you know. And I'm not getting any younger."

Sophia giggled, then cast her dark, sensuous eyes upon Tobias. "I'm ready," she breathed. "Ask me."

His heartbeat began to pound in his ears. He could scarcely hear himself when he uttered the words he had waited months to say.

"Sophia, may I have your hand in marriage?"

Sophia opened her mouth to answer, but Tobias was in a delirium of ecstasy. His feelings poured forth like a tide. "I want not only your hand, my love. Also your wit and beauty. Your body that struggles and your mind that does not. Your heart that is warm and kind and…"

"Good grief," muttered Mr. Grant under his breath.

"Yes," said Sophia before Tobias could list her qualities further. "I am all yours. For better or worse. Yes, Tobias." She flung her arms around his shoulders.

"Well, that's settled, then," declared Mr. Grant. But he was roundly ignored. Tobias stood, drawing Sophia up with him. He swung her in his arms, dancing in a circle, until she laughed and told him to put her down.

Mr. Grant cleared his throat. "Yes, well, I think I shall fetch your siblings to hear the news from your own lips. I shan't be long."

The moment Mr. Conrad had stepped outside his study, Tobias reached his hand beneath his beloved's shapely chin and lifted it gently. "Oh, how I love you…" he murmured.

"How do you love me?" Sophia whispered back.

"Shall I count the ways?" he teased.

"Just show me."

His warm breath met hers. Their lips parted and received the yearning of the other. Pleasure washed over them.

A soft giggle jerked them apart.

Bess stood in the doorway, hand over mouth, her eyes twinkling with amusement. George came up behind her.

"They were kissing," Bess announced unabashedly.

"Were they, indeed?" George replied. "And high time too, I say." He stepped forward and shook Tobias's hand. "You are a brave man to take on a force like Sophia. Just the sort of brother we need in the family."

"Oh, pooh!" cried Bess. "You men already outnumber us. We need more women in our ranks."

"Perhaps you will have your wish, Bess, now that Sophia has cleared the way for us all."

At last, the Grant family had a wedding to celebrate. They were as planets, circling the orbit of the radiant couple. For Tobias, his world was now complete. He sighed contentedly, his eyes never swerving from his precious love. And when Sophia returned his gaze, without fear or hesitation, he knew all would be well.

CHAPTER TWENTY-SIX

To wait a month seemed like an eternity. But Papa had insisted on having the banns read so that all would know their happy news.

Sophia thought the days would crawl by. All she wanted now was to be with Tobias. No more worry. No more secrets.

Well, maybe just the one. She had been preparing a little surprise, with Katie as her willing accomplice. Sophia did not even tell Adriana when she and Freddy came to visit. It was enough to see the family whole again. She did not need to draw attention to her little project.

She almost let the truth slip out with Tobias. He was so observant; it was hard to hide anything from him. So, she talked about Italy. And distracted him with kisses. It was very effective.

In the end, the month was full and glorious and a wonderful prelude for all that lay ahead.

When the day finally arrived, Sophia felt strangely calm. She did one more check that her trousseau was ready and all her papers were carefully bound in their leather portfolio. Her bonnet and a light coat lay waiting on the bed.

Katie brushed her hair. They had discussed twisting daisies into her strands, but Sophia was afraid the bonnet would crush them. Besides, her dress was cheerful enough—a grass-green muslin with white lace trim about the neck and shoulders. It matched her dark looks and the renewed freshness of her spirit. She felt young—girlish, even.

All the way to church that summer morning, she flexed her feet in the carriage. Her father merely thought she was nervous. She knew better. After all, there was nothing about marrying Tobias that brought any sensation other than joyous anticipation. But her feet must be ready, and strong.

Papa descended the carriage and helped Bess down first. Then he beckoned to the footman to carry Sophia into the church.

"No, Papa, I can manage."

Her father looked dubious. "Let me at least help you down the steps." He took her by the waist and lifted her lightly through the air, setting her down carefully. He waited until she had steadied herself before he let go. But he did not step back.

"Do not worry, Papa, I can stand on my own two feet. I've been practicing." She looked at the long path to the church entrance. "Perhaps, though, I might not mind leaning upon you a little."

"It would be my privilege," he replied, tucking her hand into his elbow and wrapping it with his own. But he remained somewhat distracted. "It is a long distance to Italy," he murmured, patting her hand absentmindedly. "And you are likely to push yourself too hard. Are you certain it is for the best? We could take care of you until his lordship and your husband return."

Sophia turned to face her father. "I am strong enough, Papa. You will see. And I will write to you every day to share all the adventures I am having. You will be assured of my wellbeing. Even a little amazed, I should think."

Her father squeezed her hand. "I am sufficiently amazed already. There is no need to prove yourself to me."

Sophia looked up towards the church entrance. It was a portal to her new life—one in which she could be fully herself. Papa was right. There was nothing more to prove, just a life to be lived, and lived well.

Her brothers had preceded them on horseback and were already seated inside, but a handful of people waited outside the door to greet the bride. As Sophia took her first steps, Adriana hastened toward her.

"Fee! It is too far. You will tire before you reach the building."

"I feel fine, Deedee. But you may walk with me if you wish. Though I daresay your condition is more fragile than mine."

Adriana blushed and touched her hand to her belly. "It is scarcely a bump yet. How did you know?"

"Freddy has been beaming like the cat that got the cream." Sophia indicated toward him with her head. "Though you could have waited until I came back from Italy. I will be sorry to miss the arrival of your little one."

"Well, I hope to be there to welcome yours."

"One thing at a time," replied Sophia, stopping to catch her breath. She looked toward the door, estimating the distance that remained to pace herself. "Is that Lord Carthige with Freddy and the vicar?"

Bess piped up. "He seems very solemn. He is nothing like your lovely Tobias, Fee. Are they really related?"

"Oh, he is harmless," Adriana answered, leaning in a bit closer to whisper. "Though the vicar might disagree. The earl has been chewing his ear off about the passage for today's service and how—did he know?—the translation from the Greek leaves much to be desired." She grinned. "It is just as well you know your classical languages so well, Fee. No doubt your new household will be filled with lively debate."

"I would enjoy that, I think," said Sophia, panting a little.

As they neared the entrance, Lord Carthige detached himself from the small gathering and strode smartly up to the bride. He offered a stiff bow, his hand upon his heart.

"Miss Grant. An honor. Mr. Grant, my sincere congratulations."

"Thank you, my lord," Sophia's father answered. "I'm afraid I have not been much of a neighbor to you, or anyone, for that matter."

"It is nothing," Lord Carthige replied kindly. "I've been told I am an even greater hermit than yourself. But I shall not mind if the new lady of the house wishes to have guests. As long as I am not expected to receive them. My library and my study are sufficient for my needs. Mr. and Mrs. Mannerly may make what they want of the rest. During my lifetime, at least."

"Do you hear that, Fee?" Adriana nudged Sophia. "Mrs. Mannerly is to be lady of the house."

"Mrs. Mannerly is yet to be made," their father reminded them. "Let's get you all inside before her husband-to-be wonders what has become of her."

Freddy collected Adriana, and Lord Carthige offered his arm to young Bess. Sophia imagined it took every ounce of restraint for Bess not to squeal with delight. The vicar waited for them to find their seats, then he gestured for Sophia to enter.

She turned to her father. "I must do this on my own, Papa."

He patted her hand, then wiped a stray tear from his eye. "I believe you can do anything you set your mind to. But I will still be here whenever you need me." He reached over and kissed her brow. One last squeeze of her hand, and he set her free.

At the far end of the church, Tobias waited, his eyes trained on the door. The moment Sophia's father walked away from her, Tobias began to rush forward, ready to take his place. Then he pulled up, as if by invisible reins. He folded his hands in front of him and waited.

Sophia took a deep breath, placing one foot gingerly in front of the other. It was perhaps twenty paces between them. They happened in complete silence. She felt buoyed up by a wave of encouraging thoughts that flowed from all present. Her eyes remained on Tobias as each step took her closer to him. She could see him almost vibrating with the urge to help her, and yet he stood still. With each step, she was more sure of herself, more certain of the man she was walking toward.

At last, they were but a breath apart.

"You beautiful miracle!" he exclaimed, just loudly enough for her to hear. "I always knew there was nothing you couldn't do. I am such a lucky…"

Sophia quickly put her finger upon his lips. "Your miracle is about to collapse in the aisle. Help me to a seat by the altar."

Together, they covered the last few steps. Sophia sank into the chair with some relief. Tobias did not release her hand.

"I am all right," she whispered up at him. "You can let go now."

"I have no intention of letting go," he answered. "Not now. Not ever."

"Good."

Tobias smiled down at her. She leaned her cheek against the back of his hand.

Yes, she thought as he caressed her skin softly with his thumb, *it is all so very, very good.* And if the rest of her life was anything like this one moment, nothing could be better.

EPILOGUE

T HE SEPTEMBER SUN shone brightly upon Rome, and the Spanish Steps in particular, coating their marbled form in a creamy hue. Tobias stepped out onto the balcony of their second-story villa, overlooking the midpoint of the steps where they curved and divided. The table had been laid for breakfast. Sophia was dusting the flakes of a croissant from her fingers. His uncle was sipping coffee and working his way through a small pile of correspondence.

"Is there anything left for me?" Tobias teased as he pulled a chair up as close to his wife as he could without crowding her.

Sophia's eyes, like the rest of her, lit up at his nearness. Her cheeks, tanned and rosy from her recent weeks outdoors, plumped with good food and wine, creased into a wide smile.

"I have buttered a croissant for you," she said, "but did not want to pour your coffee, lest it get cold. Shall I do so now?"

Tobias gathered her hand to his lips. "Are these the fingers that will pour for me?" he asked while planting kisses upon them.

"Not if you hold them ransom." She laughed. But she did not pull them away.

"Perhaps I am not thirsty yet." He held her gaze, his mouth shifting to the inside of her wrist. He felt the current pass between them. The moist tip of his tongue tasted her skin. The fine hairs on her arm stiffened.

"Ahem." Uncle Edmund cleared his throat. "I thought to visit the Villa Medici before the day grew too warm. It is the official residence of a number of sculptors and painters, studying the great masters. Are you interested in joining me?"

He directed the question to Tobias only. The route would take them up the famous steps and onward up the hill—too much exertion for Sophia, although she had grown stronger and was walking shorter distances with great confidence.

"I do not like to leave Sophia alone too long," Tobias answered.

"Perhaps we could cover the distance in stages," Sophia suggested. "I could rest on the steps and catch my breath. It will take longer, but I would like to try."

"I will leave that up to the two of you to work out," said Uncle Edmund. "But we should start as soon as possible. I will be ready once I have done with these." He indicated the letters before him.

"Is that the Howell crest?" Tobias asked, inspecting the unopened correspondence while Sophia, whose hands were free once again, poured his coffee.

"It is," his uncle confirmed, removing the seal and folding open the page. He read in silence while Tobias sipped his coffee and watched the occasional pedestrian traverse the Spanish Steps barely twenty yards from them. The pergola above the balcony was draped in vines and festooned with hanging baskets, some still in flower, providing a measure of privacy from which to watch the world without being watched in turn.

"Is he well?" Tobias eventually asked as his uncle placed the letter back upon the table.

"That depends on how you look at it, I suppose," Uncle Edmund answered. "As you know, he had no joy from any of the introductions at the poetry reading. So he has taken matters into his own hands. A rather drastic action, from what he tells me."

"That sounds ominous," commented Sophia. "What has he done?"

"Apparently, he was made aware of a suitable candidate at a dinner he attended. The young lady is out in society in name only. Her father has great ambitions for her and does not permit her to loiter among regular gentlemen at dances or gatherings of a social nature. He intends to handpick her husband."

Sophia shook her head. "Her father appears scarcely better than mine was. It seems she will move from ownership under her father to a similar fate with whichever husband he chooses. Poor girl!"

Tobias considered the news. "I don't understand. How is she more qualified than the ladies he was introduced to at the Grants'? He hasn't even met her."

"That," explained his uncle, "is apparently the very element that encourages him. Her sheltered life gives him hope that she will be unlike so many of the ladies of Munro, who, as you know, rarely act like ladies at all. He is counting on her to be untainted by their influence."

"That's all very well, but how will he go about the courtship? We're not there to assist with a meeting. And he is not what one might call confident in such matters. What are his plans?" Tobias scoffed. "To woo her through her father?"

"Er, yes." Uncle Edmund put up a defensive hand. "I know, I know. You can't imagine such a soulless route to marriage. But not all men have your passionate conviction, Nephew. Some merely survive. He needs a wife, preferably one who will at least be a little kind. And Miss Trenton's father will happily accept a wealthy viscount for his daughter. It is a question of negotiation at this point."

"He's not even going to write to her?" Sophia remembered the letter that had changed her life.

"It seems not."

"She might offer him more than mere kindness if he did," Sophia insisted.

"You are probably right"—Uncle Edmund sighed—"but that is not the route he has chosen. One can only hope that Miss

Trenton is ready for the challenges of an arranged marriage. Perhaps it is for the best. They can discover each other and build their relationship in the privacy of their shared home. Lord Howell has not had that advantage before. All his previous efforts have been in the public eye, and the constant scrutiny has been tortuous."

"Well, we wish them the very best," said Tobias, reaching for Sophia's hand once again. "I am grateful our own challenges are a thing of the past."

"Or at least limited to climbing the Spanish Steps." Sophia grinned, a now familiar glint of mischief in her eye.

"Shall we make a start, then?" inquired Uncle Edmund. "It already grows warm. I shall finish my correspondence later."

Sophia sent Katie to collect better shoes for walking, and a parasol to shield her mistress from the extremes of the Italian sun. The four of them bundled out by the ground floor entrance and turned right to ascend the steps. Sophia, leaning on Tobias's arm as much for affection as support, took the stairs slowly, so as to pace herself. Their uncle walked ahead with his long stride, waiting patiently when he drew level to the balcony where they had talked and dined but a few minutes before.

When Tobias, Sophia, and Katie—*avec parasol*—caught up to him, Sophia was ready to rest.

"I fear it is already growing hot." Uncle Edmund fretted. "The entire expedition is upward, even beyond the steps. Perhaps we should resume this outing tomorrow. We could start earlier. Or hire a trap to take Sophia the long way around."

Tobias saw the disappointment in Sophia's face. She hated a fuss. And she was just as keen as the rest of them to visit the famed art academe.

"That won't be necessary," he replied. He put his arms around his wife and whispered, "Hold on tight." Then he lifted her up, as if once again carrying her over the threshold. They ascended the steps together, Sophia nestled against his shoulder, her gentle breath on his neck.

The heat of the day did not compare to the warmth in his heart as he climbed steadily onward, his beloved safely in his arms. Onward to their day together. Onward to their lives together. And when Sophia kissed him on the tender skin beneath his ear, he felt he could climb on and up to the moon and stars, his lover against his breast, his happiness complete.

Author's Notes

Sophia's Letter, a Regency novel, was inspired by the romance between Elizabeth Barrett Browning and Robert Browning—one of the most heartbreaking and heartwarming true love stories of the Victorian era.

Elizabeth Barrett was a lively, intelligent child, the eldest of twelve. She was something of a social introvert, however, and delved into books as a diversion. She was widely read in multiple languages and corresponded with learned men on literature and philosophy. Struck by a mysterious illness in her teens, she became an invalid for the remainder of her life. Her main consolation was her family and her desire to be a poet recognized by her peers.

Robert Browning, a succcssful poet in his own right, became enthralled with her writing and, soon after, with Elizabeth herself. It took him months to convince her to allow him a visit, but only because she preferred writing letters to mixing with society. His persistence paid off, however. They discovered they had much in common, which drew them closer.

But it was their differences that really sparked the relationship. Elizabeth, despite her distaste for socializing, was a deeply passionate person. Robert, on the other hand, was outwardly boisterous, without revealing his innermost self. He wanted to be more like her. In return, he offered her admiration and acceptance without sway. For the first time since her mother's death, she felt loved for who she was. Robert's love was unconditional.

In contrast, her father had harsh rules for Elizabeth and her siblings. Though her illness and her mother's death were unconnected, Mr. Barrett did become obsessed with keeping his children with him. He ultimately forbade them to marry, threatening to disown and disinherit them if they did.

Elizabeth was torn between the tender memory of her father as he once had been and the tyrant he had become. She never found the courage to face her father. At the age of forty, she married in secret, bringing his wrath upon her. He carried out his threat, disinheriting Elizabeth and never speaking to her ever again. Even some of her brothers felt betrayed and would not speak to her for a long time afterward. Her sister Arabella—who was also involved in a secret romance but never married—remained in regular contact with her.

Wilson, Elizabeth's loyal lady's maid, traveled with her to Italy and helped to raise the Brownings' only son, whose nickname was Pen. Despite the initial pain caused by the loss of her family, Elizabeth and Robert Browning were happy and in love until her death fifteen years later.

Acknowledgements

Writing is largely a solitary occupation. However, there are a whole host of people without whom I would never have come this far. People who have believed in me, encouraged my literary pursuits, and offered great advice with my craft.

My mom has been with me on my writing journey from the start. Not only is she gifted in her own right, but she has been a loyal supporter every step of the way. I love that we can talk about the ups and downs of writing and publishing on a regular basis. Thank you, *Mamma*. You're the best!

My husband is my biggest fan. Even though he prefers to study massive tomes on business or engineering, he will make time to read my fiction and not fall asleep while doing it. Bless his heart!

Carri Kühn and Bex Drate, where would I be without you? Your courage in your own writing adventures has been contagious. So often I have asked you to "take a quick look" at my query letters or last-minute edits when I've lost faith in myself! You will never truly know how much you have meant to me.

To my editor and the rest of the team at Dragonblade, thank you for taking a chance on me, guiding me, and being like family to me. I feel so blessed that you look out for your authors the way you do.

Last, but definitely not least, my deepest thanks to all my readers, whether they be friends, family, or lovely strangers who enjoy my words. You are the reason these pages exist.

About the Author

Elizabeth Donne writes sweet Regency romance, a natural outpouring of a lifelong love affair with English literature.

She has spent most of her life in Cape Town, South Africa. In 2015, she moved to Iowa with her husband, their two children, two cats, and their African bush dog. When she's not writing, or discovering the secret wonders of the Midwest, she is enthusiastically introducing her visitors to the joys of drinking *rooibos* tea. With a biscuit, of course.

www.ingramcontent.com/pod-product-compliance
Lightning Source LLC
Chambersburg PA
CBHW060445310726
48977CB00001B/329